WITH MY LAST BREATH
Copyright © 2024 by Kaye Dobbie

All rights reserved.

No part of this publication may be reproduced, distributed, or transmitted in any form or by any means, including photocopying, recording, or other electronic or mechanical methods, without the prior written permission of the copywrite owner, except as permitted by U.S. copyright law.

The story, all names, characters, and incidents portrayed in this production are fictitious. No identification with actual persons (living or deceased), places, buildings, and products is intended or should be inferred.

AI RESTRICTION: The author expressly prohibits any entity from using this publication for purposes of training artificial intelligence (AI) technologies to generate text, including without limitation technologies that are capable of generating works in the same style or genre as this publication. The author reserves all rights to license uses of this work for generative AI training and development of machine learning language models.

Cover Design & Interior Format by
The Killion Group, Inc.

With My Last Breath

AUSTRALIAN BESTSELLING AUTHOR
KAYE DOBBIE

*For my brother John
who loved to read spooky books.*

Be careful what you wish for…

ONE

Ypres, Belgium
October 1917

OWEN DUCKED LOW and ran along the front-line trench. On the other side was No Man's Land, where his fellow countrymen lay dead and dying.

"Get out of the way, you bloody fool!"

The passing soldier glared at Owen, either not noticing or ignoring his captain's insignia. War correspondents were all made up to the rank of Captain, whether they deserved it or not. The soldier was gone before Owen had a chance to ask him where he could find Major Lanyard. Owen had met the major several times at headquarters and found him to be a sensible man in a world where good sense was in short supply. They had become friends, finding common ground in their backgrounds, their sense of obligation to their country, and their dismay with the high toll of human life the war was taking on their countrymen.

Owen turned a corner. A stretcher-bearer party was ahead of him, but the two men with red crosses around their upper arms were not hurrying and the stretcher was empty. One of them reached into his jacket and pulled out a cigarette. Owen went to pass them, pushing himself hard against the trench wall.

"You in a hurry, mate?" The laconic Australian accent was no surprise in this place, where he had heard voices from every corner of the world. "The one we're off to fetch isn't going anywhere. Deserter," he added, and spat on the ground. "Major Lanyard is having him shot."

Owen swallowed his sudden nausea. Shooting deserters was meant to be a warning to others, and he imagined that especially at a time like this, when Major Lanyard was sending his men across No Man's Land to face possible death, he would want to focus his troop's attention.

It was brutal, but then war was brutal. Owen wondered how he would cope if he was ordered to run into enemy fire, and then his clever brain was twisting and turning, creating a story for his newspaper, the *London Courier*.

"Do you know where I can find Major Lanyard?" he asked.

"Up ahead. Look for the red flag."

He watched as the stretcher-bearers took a breather, puffing on their cigarettes. The deserter must have a story. Would Major Lanyard discuss it with him? There had to be a reason for him to have deserted. Owen considered the questions he might ask some of the dead chap's colleagues as he made his way forward.

A shell made the ground shake, and he felt the

first splatters of rain hit his tin helmet. He glanced up at the grey sky and saw the red flag and the shored up entry to what must be the major's bunker. A couple of soldiers were slumped against the side of the trench, as if waiting, and he recognised one of them as a corporal he had spoken with on another occasion.

"I'm here to see Major Lanyard," he said. "Owen Flett, from the *London Courier*. He's expecting me."

They stared back at him, disinterested and weary. The corporal answered. "He's not here. Had something to do. Should be back soon, he said."

Owen looked further down the trench. "I can meet up with him?"

The soldiers exchanged glances. "We can't let anyone through, sorry, Captain. Orders."

The deserter, of course. As much as he wanted to be present, he couldn't disobey an order. All the same, he had the makings of a story and he may as well start his interview now.

"When you say he had something to do… Is that the deserter?"

The two men exchanged a glance and the corporal shrugged. "Aye. The men were ordered to watch him shot before they went over, just to encourage them, like."

Owen reached into his pocket, found his cigarette case and offered it to the two men. They both took a cigarette, tucking them away for later. "Do you know anything about the man?"

"That one is a right bastard," the private muttered. "I mean, some of them you feel sorry for, you have to. You understand why they do it. But him…" He grimaced.

The corporal nodded in agreement. "World's better off without 'im."

Owen felt a glimmer of excitement. Maybe there was a story that was worth pursuing here, a different kind of grim misery?

"So he wasn't… isn't just a deserter?"

Another look exchanged by the two men. "No, it was more than that."

He had been about to ask the man's name when voices drifted from further along the trench. Owen took a step and then paused, expecting the two soldiers to stop him, but they simply shrugged and turned away.

Owen squinted against the mist that seemed to have risen up around him. Was that Major Lanyard's voice? He took another step.

There was a crack of gunfire. Was the firing squad closer than he'd thought? Should he go back? And then a scream came from above him, the high-pitched whine of a shell, so close he could feel the air around him heat, scorching his skin. Then a roar. The feeling of falling, of being crushed.

Then nothing.

Slowly, he became aware of small sensations. The weight of his body, held down, buried. The smell of damp earth and blood. Muted voices drifting further and further away.

Emilia. He had to get home to Emilia. His heart pounded so loud he could no longer hear anything apart from that rattle in his chest. It stuttered, stopped, started again. And then stopped altogether. Nothing now but endless silence.

Eventually, it was panic that forced his eyes to open. He wasn't sure how much time had passed, but he'd expected to see the trench or the ruined landscape of Belgium. Instead, he was seated on a bench in a railway station.

It was so bizarre, so incongruous, that his first thought was that he was gravely injured and hallucinating. He stared as shadowy people wandered past him. Men in uniform. Steam hissed from a train waiting at the platform, the acrid smell filling his nostrils. Soldiers were boarding and he watched as the conductor took their tickets, closely inspecting each one. Several passengers were turned away. A protesting private began to sob.

How had he arrived here? Where *was* here? He had been to many train stations all over Europe and although this one did not look familiar to him, that meant nothing. They all blurred into something similar after a while. He listened hard to the voices around him, in case that gave him a clue, but the languages were a mish-mash of English, French, German, and many others he didn't recognise.

He was still unconscious. He must be. Hallucinating, maybe. Perhaps he was injured and lying in the hospital tent behind the front line? Perhaps he was on his way home?

Owen looked down at himself, expecting to see injuries, but he appeared to be unhurt. No wounds, no limbs missing, none of the horrible gaping holes that a shell or machine guns could inflict. It seemed nothing was missing apart from his memory.

As he sat there, confused, his thoughts slipping in and out of the moment, he tried to grab onto the familiar. The past.

Before he left England, he and Emilia had visited her home in Belsham. Owen and Emilia's father, Maurice Honeywell, the well-known writer of crime novels, had sat comfortably together in front of the fire. They'd been pondering various misdeeds and how they could be solved and the perpetrators brought to justice, without giving the game away in the first paragraph. Owen often thought that if he hadn't become a journalist, he might have been an author.

As his memories grew stronger, the smells of the train station, steam and coal and fear, receded. Now he could feel the warmth of that fire, hear the crackle of the flames, taste the warmth of brandy in his throat.

"You two." Emilia's teasing, loving voice crept into his head. He looked up and she was smiling down at him, a tray with two cups of tea and two slices of cake in her hands. "Now Dad has enough ideas for at least fifty more books. I don't mind helping when the setting is near home, but please, no more crimes in Cairo."

Emilia was her father's researcher and fact checker, and often complained, in a tongue in cheek sort of way, about some of the more obscure places he'd needed her to research.

Her father was trying not to smile. "I thought perhaps I would set my next book in Siberia."

"In winter, I suppose?" She laughed, and her beautiful eyes, her kind brown eyes, warmed.

Emelia. His wife, his love, the woman he'd left at home to wait for him while he went off to a war he didn't believe in to sate his need for honesty and integrity. Was that selfless or selfish?

His thoughts drifted to his final night in London, he and Evie cuddled together in bed in his house in Easton Street. "You can't change the world," she'd whispered in the darkness.

"I can try."

"I suppose you can. But if you don't come back this time… Being without you … that would change my world, Owen."

It was more than she usually said. She was brave, stoic, and up until now she had always sent him off with a smile. This time, her eyes were bright with tears and her mouth trembled. He felt a sliver of fear. Because he had to go, they both knew it, and she was making it more difficult than it needed to be. He had begun to understand why some men did not come home at all, but spent their leave at headquarters away from family and friends who would only make the return to war all the more difficult.

"We'll take a holiday when I get back," he'd said, needing her to be strong so that he could be strong. "Where would you like to go? Scotland?"

She took a shaky breath. "Scotland is rather far away," she said. "Isle of Wight might be better." As she went on, her voice grew in strength, until it was almost back to normal. The conversation meandered on, and the awkward moment passed.

When it came time for him to say goodbye, he'd held her close and she didn't weep. She smiled bravely, just as he'd wanted her to, so that his heart didn't rip in two in his desire to be two men at once.

Selfish and selfless.

Owen wasn't sure how long he sat, lost in the past, staring out at the station and the movement all around him. The train had gone, but there was another one waiting. A conductor stood nearby. He was tall and thin, in the usual sort of uniform conductors wore. His skin wasn't just pale, however, it was white. Deathly white. He stared at Owen with the darkest eyes he'd ever seen. Something compelled Owen to stand and move toward him.

"Have you a ticket?" the conductor asked. Owen didn't recognise the accent. He searched in his jacket pocket, expecting to find a slip of paper, but there was nothing. He searched again while the conductor waited.

"I don't have one," he said at last.

The man's dark eyes fixed on Owen. "You can't board without a ticket," he said. The sound of a throat clearing. Someone was standing behind him, and Owen turned. A soldier, smelling of damp wool and regret, stood behind him. The conductor held out his hand, and the soldier gave him a ticket. The man brushed by Owen to climb aboard, but Owen clasped his arm to stop him.

"Where are you going?" he asked. "Are we

being transferred? Is the war over?"

The man stared at him with a blank expression, and, without a word, he pulled away from Owen's grip and climbed aboard. The conductor firmly closed the door and blew his whistle. Owen stumbled back as the train sent out a burst of steam and began to move, slowly gaining speed as it left the platform.

Owen turned back to the bench and sat down. Maybe the next train would be his. Maybe then he could go home.

Another man was seated nearby, his head bowed, muttering to himself. At least Owen wasn't alone in his wait.

Emilia, he thought. Had he really been torn between being selfish and selfless? Suddenly the idea of telling the truth for the masses and having his name on a by-line did not matter nearly as much as being with his wife.

Emilia.

He pressed his palm to his chest and he felt more alone than he ever had in his entire life.

A pair of shiny shoes stopped in front of him and when he looked up there was a bearded man watching him. He half smiled and spoke.

"Mr Flett. I have an offer I'd like to make you."

Notice in the *London Courier*, November 1917

Flett, Captain Owen. War Correspondent for this newspaper. Missing, presumed dead.

Captain Flett was working as a war correspondent for the *Courier* when the trench he was in was hit by a German shell. His body was not found, but he is presumed dead.

It appears that, not content to sit back and have the news from the front brought to him, Captain Flett had travelled into the trenches to speak to the soldiers himself. It was his belief that the readers at home preferred their information straight from the mouths of those doing the fighting, something frowned upon by the military hierarchy.

A man known for his integrity and firm beliefs, Captain Flett will be greatly missed by his colleagues.

He leaves behind his wife, Emilia, daughter of crime writer M V Honeywell, and a younger sister Florence, as well as the many friends and colleagues who will mourn his passing.

TWO

London
March 1919

THE BUS MOVED forward, and I tried to make myself smaller in my seat as a large man squeezed in beside me. We didn't speak, and we both wore face masks, so there wasn't any need to be polite. I was glad of that. This was one of my sad days.

It was because I was thinking of Owen, although there wasn't ever a day when I *didn't* think of Owen. Sometimes I pleaded with God, promising anything, everything, if only I could have him back again. At times, the weight was so heavy that I wondered how I could get through all those empty hours ahead of me. This was one of those days.

It was ages since I had been to London, and now I was beginning to see familiar places. We had spent our short married life here, at the house in Easton Street. Every corner the bus turned brought forth a memory or reminded me of one. My father's cottage in the country, where we had first met, was painful enough, but there were other memories there to distract myself with. In London, there was only us.

The man beside me rose and got off at his stop, and a woman took his place. Winter was holding on, and the cold rainy weather meant that the bus was filled with passengers of all ages. A baby bawled toward the front and I could see its mother desperately rock it. Despite the protective mask I wore over my nose and mouth, I could smell damp wool competing with the disinfectant which was supposed to keep the influenza at bay.

The numbers of deaths had been dropping since last year when they had been so frighteningly high, but then over winter had come a new wave of fatalities. Now that the war was over, troops returning home had brought the infection with them. The community had been warned to remain vigilant, and the government was doing its best to check the spread of the disease in public places.

I had escaped infection, staying with my father in his cottage in Belsham, near Cambridge. He too was well. Florence's job in the hospital brought her in contact with many influenza patients, but she had survived the worst, apart from a fortnight in bed which she said was more about her feeling sorry for herself and missing her brother.

The bus jerked to a halt as a passenger got off and two more passengers got on before it started moving again. This morning, I had started out my journey to London by taking a branch line train from my father's house, then changing at

Cambridge to the London train. Gradually the open countryside had given way to choking suburbs and then the predictably smoky gloom of Paddington Station, where I'd caught a bus. Until now I had refused Florence's invitations, but this time she would not take no for an answer.

"You never come and see me anymore! I know it must feel awkward, because you and Owen used to live in this house together, but I miss you, Emilia. I miss my brother. I miss you *both*."

The crackly phone line had not been able to hide the break in Florence's voice. A mixture of guilt and longing had won me over, and I agreed to a visit for a couple of days. A couple of days which Florence had immediately lengthened into at least a week.

"What about your job at the hospital?"

"It's voluntary," Florence had reminded me. "My real job will be to entertain you."

That made me laugh. "I can't be away for too long. My father—"

My mother had died when I was born, so it had been the two of us all of my life. As well as keeping house, I had been his assistant when it came to his writing career. I worked as his researcher. At some point, he had stopped doing his own investigating and I had taken over. So, in addition to answering his mail and typing up his manuscripts, I had the enviable task of making certain that his characters could actually do the things he said they could.

Crime novels require a certain amount of medical knowledge, as well as an understanding of police procedure. Plots had to be reasonably believable, and while sometimes my father's fans were asked to take a leap of faith, he preferred not to make that leap too broad. I sorted the details. Some of those he considered an irritation but I liked to make everything fit together neatly. I liked to think my contribution was the oil added to a machine, making it run that little bit more smoothly than it otherwise might have done. That was my reward, as well as my father's dedication in every book he had written since I was born.

"Nonsense! He can spare you for a week." Florence spoke with the confidence of a twenty-five year old woman who had always had someone to pick up the pieces for her. "I've seen him when he's deep in his writing. Unless you appeared in front of him wearing a deerstalker and false moustache, he wouldn't notice you'd gone. Oh Emilia, I wish Owen was here …"

So I had agreed to stay. Because of all the people in the world, Florence was the only one who missed him as much as I did.

I stared unseeingly at the passing scenery. London hadn't changed much since the war ended last November. Although the neglected roads were beginning to be repaired, a sense of forlorn abandonment still hung over the city. Armistice had been celebrated deliriously, people crowding into the capital despite the threat of Spanish flu, only for reality to return the next day. The war was over, the war was won, but so many men were never coming home and so many families had empty chairs around their tables. Nothing could ever be the same again, and that fact was brought home by the celebrations.

A former serviceman stood in the shelter of a brick wall, his hat held out, silently asking for money. I didn't see such things in Belsham. Those who returned to the village were taken back into their homes and their farms. But here destitution seemed to be everywhere. On my short journey from Paddington, I had seen men who had obviously been injured in the war, while others simply appeared lost, as if their bodies were in familiar surroundings but their heads were still on foreign soil.

I understood that feeling. I was lost too. When Owen died, I had lost everything that mattered to me, and although I continued to live, it wasn't truly living, because nothing made sense.

We'd been in the house in London the last time we were together, Owen on leave. His arm around me as we lay in bed, my cheek to his chest. His heart had been beating, so strong, so alive. And I'd lain there and listened to it and told myself that for it to stop was impossible.

"We should move to the country when I come back," Owen had said, stroking my hair. "Somewhere bright and clean and far away."

I'd heard it in his voice then, the trickle of despair that he tried to hide from me.

"Would the newspaper let you go?" I'd asked. "Perhaps you could start a newspaper in Belsham? *The Village Crusader*?"

He'd looked down at me, and I'd seen amusement warm his grey eyes. The quiet understanding that lay between us. Owen's moment of despair had gone, and I was glad for it. Guilty, but glad. He had confided in me about the sanitised stories he was ordered to write, the lies to keep the public blissfully ignorant of the horrors going on. The truth was something he was desperate to expose, and sometimes he even managed to instil a little bit of reality into his pieces for the *London Courier*. He'd told me how he was refusing to stay at headquarters where the other war correspondents were housed, where it was safe, that he was instead travelling to the front lines, so that he could talk to the men there. I had wanted to protest. I remembered holding my breath to stop myself from begging. 'Stay safe' had been on the tip of my tongue. 'I don't care about anyone else. Please, stay away from danger.'

But I couldn't say those selfish words, not when Owen was being so unselfish. He was a man intent on one thing, revealing the truth. I knew he would only remind me that if others were dying, then it was his duty to tell their stories.

Would he have listened to me and stayed at headquarters if I had asked? Or would he have continued to risk his life but stop being honest to me about it? At that moment I hadn't put my need for him above his moral and ethical principles as a journalist, and every day since I wished I had.

A tear spilled over my lashes. I felt its warmth on my skin, rolling along the edge of my mask, and then down my chin until it reached the fur collar of my coat. I shouldn't be crying. There was no point, just as there was no point in talking to someone who was gone. Owen had been dead for eighteen months, and there were so many other widows and fatherless children. There was already so much despair in this new, peaceful world. It seemed wrong of me to still be grieving.

I reached with a shaky hand to wipe my tears away, but they kept falling and I couldn't seem to stop them. Perhaps it was seeing the serviceman, or knowing I was going home to Owen's house, where we had lived for that short time and where we'd been happy. I wondered then if my tears were for myself as much as him.

It had been too short, our life together. It had really only begun the day Owen proposed.

August 1916

I was in London.

For the first time in my life, I was in London. Despite the bad news from the war, and the rather grim air of the city, it was summer, and the parks were green and alive with people making the most of the fine day. Being here was a miracle in itself. My father was writing a book set in the British Museum, with a murder in the Elgin saloon, where the Elgin marbles were kept. He had devised a complicated plot relating back to Greece.

The museum had been closed for several

months now. Most of the staff had been conscripted, and the artefacts taken to safety in the tunnels under London. My father was lucky in that he knew someone who could give me access to the now largely empty building. The marbles would not be there, but I could see the room, and use my imagination.

It had been my suggestion to reconnoitre for him. The truth? I had insisted. I found that I was far more determined these days. Belsham had grown too small for me, I told myself, and maybe that was so, but a big reason for my motivation was Owen. My father, though dubious of the news at first, had taken it far better than I'd expected.

Who will bring me my boiled egg and toast every morning? Who will remind me to shave? What about wood for the fire?

I laughed and told him I had arranged for a girl from the village to come and cook and clean for him, but as we parted, I wondered if he would even notice I was gone. He was writing now, and the book was at a stage when he had a tendency to vanish into the pages for days on end. I knew he loved me, but I doubted he'd miss me. Perhaps if the girl forgot to boil his egg for the necessary length of time he'd notice. I left instructions and crossed my fingers, but I wasn't about to cancel my trip.

Excitement quietly bubbled and buzzed inside me.

When Owen heard I was coming up to

London, he said he would meet me at the station. He was home for a short while before he had to return to the war again. Summer was a busy time on the front, as I knew from his grim reports in the *Courier*. So many deaths on the Somme, and poison gas attacks in Verdun. It was too much sometimes, and I wondered how he could see such things and write about them without going insane.

I will understand if you can't meet me, I'd written to him before I left.

I want to see you, he had written back. *I need to see you.*

And so I was waiting for him outside Paddington station, watching people come and go, while motor vehicles chugged by. A horse pulling a waggon seemed out of place here. A far cry from Belsham, where motor cars were rare indeed. I wasn't intimidated. In fact, a little to my surprise, I wanted more.

I felt him before I saw him. A tingle on the back of my neck, a knowing that he was there. I turned around and there he was, standing close behind me, his tie loosened and his jacket over his arm. It was a warm day and his dark hair was a little windblown, as though he'd been in a hurry. He was smiling his half smile as his grey eyes took me in, just as I took him in.

"Emilia." It was as if we had seen each other just yesterday rather than last year. "Here you are," he added when I found myself tongue tied.

Owen frowned then, his gaze moving to my cheek, and he reached out and brushed his fingers across my skin. "You had some soot," he said, "from the train. There, that's better."

I felt myself colour. I had the sort of pale complexion that coloured easily. He smiled and held out the arm without the jacket over it. "Come on," he said. "I have my car. I want to take you home to meet my sister. Give me your case."

I handed it over and tucked my hand into the crook of his elbow. We set off down the street as if we were old friends, and it was the strangest thing, but I felt as if we really were. More than that perhaps, but I kept my secret longings to myself because… well, because this was Owen Flett, and I was just a country mouse.

"I wasn't sure what to wear," I said, breathless, sounding far younger than my twenty-five years. "I've never been to London before."

He looked down at me, inspecting my matching skirt and jacket, and then back into my eyes. The corner of his mouth twitched as if he wanted to smile but was keeping it contained. "You're perfect," he said.

I think if I hadn't already been in love with him, I would have fallen in love right then.

"I've been desperate to see you," he admitted, pausing beside a length of wrought iron fencing.

"Have you?" Desperate implied a sense of urgency that I knew I felt, but for him to feel it too…

He smiled. "I have. Things have been so busy here. I was planning to drive up to Belsham to see you before I left again. Then you said you were coming to London."

"When are you leaving?"

"In a week. I was lucky to get home at all."

"A week." I must have sounded bleak. By now, I was well aware that the war wasn't something we could win with fine speeches or a few brave charges. It was bloody and brutal, and although Owen was based at headquarters with the other correspondents, I worried about him.

As if he had read my mind—and he seemed to be rather good at that—he said, "They keep us journalists well away from the fighting. Well, they try to. I feel like I'm missing a lot. How can I tell the truth when I'm so removed from the battle lines?"

Owen had spoken of this before. He wanted to see what was happening with his own eyes, and hear from the men in the thick of it. I knew it was only a matter of time before he got his way.

"I can't wait to read your next piece in the *Courier*. They are so much more real than the others." He emphasized with the fighting men as if he was there among them. It occurred to me that he may not be telling me the whole truth when he said he was at headquarters. Suddenly I was terrified that he would be killed alongside the men whose stories he told.

"Emilia?"

I started. He was talking and I hadn't heard a word. He touched my hand and began again.

"Being there, seeing death close at hand… it has turned my thoughts in a direction they've never taken before."

"Every night I pray you stay safe."

"Thank you," he said, still watching me.

I waited, not sure what he wanted to say. Across the street, some children were playing, noisy and unaware.

He bit his lip. "Emilia. I haven't been able to forget you since the moment I met you. Every day I look forward to your letters. When one doesn't arrive, I feel quite bereft. I feel as if you've burrowed your way into my chest, a warm little bundle beside my heart."

Not the most romantic statement, perhaps. 'A warm little bundle' rather than him being slain by my beauty and wit, and yet it melted me.

"Owen," I whispered, not knowing what to say. He was so much better at expressing himself than I was.

And then he stunned me.

"I wish to marry you before I go back," he said. "Will you marry me, Emilia?"

The sun shined on his hair, and his hand was warm where it held mine. His eyes were filled with longing and love. The man, and the moment, was perfect. There was only one thing I could say.

"Yes. I will."

His shoulders sagged with relief and he gave a soft huff of laughter. "Thank God," he said. "If you'd said no, I don't know what I would have done. Cry, probably."

He leaned down and kissed me, right there on the street, in front of the pedestrians and traffic. A Cockney newspaper boy on the corner whistled and cooed.

I felt myself soar. I felt so fierce. A loud roar of

longing and desire and want, all tangled together on that London street. At the same time, I wondered if Owen Flett would be my destruction, because a love like this could never be found a second time, could never be recovered from.

March, 1919

The bus jerked, its engine groaning as it made another stop. I had my face turned to the window, not wanting to share my grief with the woman sitting beside me. I felt the seat move as she got to her feet. A moment later, something was pressed into my gloved hand, and her fingers gave mine a squeeze.

I looked up, startled, forgetting that I was meant to be hiding my tears. Bright blue eyes above an influenza mask gazed down at me. There was grey in the brown hair curling from beneath her hat, and her coat was struggling to stay buttoned over plump breasts and wide hips. She nodded toward my hand in a way that seemed meaningful and then leaned down. I could smell her perfume—English Fern.

"He wants to speak to you," she whispered.

"Pardon?"

The stranger nodded encouragingly, her gaze darting to what she had put in my hand. "Come tonight," she said, then turned and made her way down the aisle to the door.

I stared after her, then looked down at my hand.

There was a folded piece of printed paper there, and I straightened it out on my lap.

> *The World Beyond Spiritualist Church is holding a meeting at No. 7 Tottenham Court Road, 7pm to 10pm.*
>
> *Only members of the church and those with a serious interest in communicating with the departed will be admitted.*
>
> *Medium, Miss Anna Ward, will endeavour to pass on messages to those present.*

Disappointed, I lay my palm over the words, covering them up. There were so many of these people these days, seeking out the vulnerable. The tidal wave of grief the country felt had brought with it a desperate need to contact those who had died. And what better way than in a seance, where messages were delivered from the dead to the living? Sometimes there were amazing 'appearances' by the loved one wearing a white shroud.

It was easy to be sceptical, but really, was it so terrible to give hope to those who needed it? So long as there were no suspicious requests for hundreds of pounds, what did it matter, and why should I begrudge them the comfort they sought? A bereaved mother or wife, a mourning father or son. For one moment, they could believe their loved one was happy and safe, living in paradise. Was it so very different from the empty platitudes offered by the churches or their talk of heaven and angels?

The postmistress in Belsham had been to a seance in Cambridge only last week. She'd beckoned me when I went to post one of Father's letters, and insisted that Owen had spoken to the gathering and that the medium had even described him.

'Tall, dark haired, handsome man in uniform with grey eyes and an uneven smile. It was him, Emilia, I know it!'

There was another meeting the next week, and she said I should come with her, that Owen had a message for me, but I hadn't gone. I couldn't bring myself to accept that sort of false comfort. I knew what would happen if I went to the meeting. My 'husband' would appear and tell me how wonderful his life now was, how he felt no resentment or regrets. The typical stuff the bereaved were dished out. But it was all a lie.

The man I loved wouldn't utter such pap. He would be full of fire at the injustices in the world, raging that he had been taken from this life before his time, and worried about me being left alone. Even death could not wipe clean those traits that were essentially Owen. If I had to listen to lies, then it would be as if I had lost him all over again. The first time in the cold Belgium soil and the second in some cosy suburban sitting room.

The truth was that the medium in Cambridge, just like the woman on the bus, probably told everyone who looked lost that there was a message waiting for them.

I tightened my hand into a fist until the flyer was a scrunched up ball. The bus began to slow again. Looking up, I saw I was finally at my stop. I pulled down my case and hurried for the door, stumbling over an old woman's bag of knitting, before I clattered down the steps and onto the street. The wind was gusting, indifferent to my shivers, and I reached up to tug down my hat.

He wants to speak to you.

Unable to help myself, I opened my hand and looked at the ball of paper. I should let it drop, let the wind take it away. And yet... if there was the slightest chance that Owen was waiting to speak to me, I should take it. Shouldn't I?

With a groan of frustration, I closed my hand over the printed words and made my way with brisk steps toward the street corner. Behind me, I heard the bus engine grumble as it moved on to the next top.

What if life and death wasn't anything like the churchgoers believed? No cosy heaven, no threat of hell. What if it was like that bus, and while everyone climbed aboard, some people got off early while others stayed on for a longer ride. For a little while, Owen and I had been riding together, but he had got off and now it was only me. Left behind. I couldn't bring myself to believe he was ever going to appear to me in a white sheet.

I looked down at the ball of paper again, then opened my fingers and let it drop.

THREE

I STOOD ON THE front step and looked up at the house in Easton Street.

The house had three stories and gables, an elegant town house that would have fit nicely into any Jane Austen novel. It had been left to Owen and Florence by their parents, but Owen had lived here, at first alone, and then with me for a time. After he was killed, Florence had moved in while I went back home to my father in Belsham.

There used to be a couple of servants who did things like open the door and admit visitors, but since the war times had changed beyond all recognition. Who wanted a poorly paid job cleaning someone else's house when there were far more opportunities available? People's eyes had been opened and they could never go back to the world their parents and grandparents had inhabited. Being in service was no longer a matter of pride but a drudgery too awful to be borne.

I had barely knocked twice when the door opened.

"Emilia!" Florence flung herself into my arms. I was engulfed in a cloud of perfume and realised at that moment how much I had missed my glamorous sister-in-law. Being here and seeing her also brought back so many memories of Owen, creating a sickening tug of war between joy and sorrow, but I had missed her.

Florence stepped back at last and her eyes, Owen's eyes, were bright with tears. Her silk blouse was the colour of a winter sunset and she wore an ankle length pleated skirt. She always made me feel dowdy, though I had never resented it. Both she and Owen were effortlessly charming and good-looking, and I accepted I was very much the provincial mouse living in their shadow.

I noticed the scarf over her head. "What have you done to yourself?"

"I wanted you to be the first to see," Florence replied, closing the door behind me and taking my case out of my hand. She led the way inside and I trailed after her.

"See what?"

Everything here was the same. Familiar paintings still hung on the wall, and the polished refectory table had a vase of flowers on top, next to an untidy bundle of mail Florence had yet to read. An old velvet covered armchair that Owen had said belonged to a great grandparent who bred spaniels, and still smelled of dog.

The place was rather less tidy than it used to be, but Florence had never pretended to be domestic. We went into the sitting room, my favourite place, with its overstuffed sofa and old leather armchairs covered in an eclectic collection of cushions. The bookshelves overflowed with old favourites mixed among the first editions, as if the importance of a book was in the pleasure it gave rather than its monetary or literary value. The curtains were already drawn against the darkening afternoon and a lamp was on, throwing a warm yellow light across the room.

I noticed a familiar photo on the mantelpiece. It had been taken on the steps of the village church in Belsham after our wedding. Owen was looking down at me in the curve of his arm, while I beamed at the camera. So happy. So much happiness captured in that single moment.

Florence was unwrapping her head and couldn't see how close I was to tears. And then I forgot to be sad because my brunette sister-in-law had gone auburn.

"Ta-dah!" she said, spinning around.

"It looks…"

Florence cocked her head. "You loathe it."

"No, I don't." And I didn't. "You look lovely. Different, that's all."

Florence smiled at me. "Sometimes different is what you need in life," she said. Her grey eyes dropped down to my hand. "What do you have there?"

I opened my fingers and stared at the crumpled ball of paper. After I'd dropped it outside in the street, it had simply lain there at my feet. The bitter wind that had tugged at my clothing had died away. For reasons I chose not to understand, I couldn't bear to leave it.

"Something someone gave me on the bus," I said, trying to pretend it didn't matter.

"Was it someone begging for money? They all

do it." She had turned to the drinks trolley. "Can I pour you anything? It's not too early, is it?" She glanced at the clock on the mantel beside the wedding photograph.

"A little, perhaps."

She came back, gently removing the paper from my hand and smoothing it out on the back of the sofa. I saw the frown between her winged eyebrows. "I didn't think you were one for spiritualism," she said cautiously. Her gaze was sharp. "Are you going to this?"

"No. I wasn't… I don't think so." I sighed and sat down on one of the chairs, hearing the crackle of old leather. "It's complicated."

"Tell me."

I told her what the woman had said on the bus, and Florence informed me that she probably said that to every stranger. Then I told her about the postmistress in the village. "I don't believe Owen will be there," I said quietly. "But if I don't go … if I let my prejudices stop me from going and then he… I know I'll be disappointed and it will all be bunkum, but at least I'll *know* it's bunkum."

"Owen didn't believe in an afterlife."

"He joked about preferring the old Norse idea of Valhalla. All those wonderful banquets." I laughed, but it sounded more like a sob.

Florence sat on the arm of the chair, putting her arm around me. "I understand. You can't help but wish that maybe it's true, and Owen is going to speak to you. You want to test the hypothesis, and once you prove it's twaddle, you can let it go."

I nodded, grateful that she could put my jumbled thoughts into words.

"I'll come with you," she said firmly.

I blinked at her. "You don't have to."

"I want to." She stood up. "We can go to Bambini's first. Make a night of it."

Bambini's had been Owen's favourite place too, when we lived here together. We often went there after he finished for the day, drinking cheap chianti and talking about the world. Painful as it all was, this might be what I needed right now. To remind myself of the real Owen, the flesh and blood man I had loved, and not the watered-down imitation I was sure would be dished up at the seance.

Florence looked at me sideways as she sipped her gin and tonic, and I wondered what she was thinking. Perhaps that I was a poor, frail thing that a strong wind might blow away. That I had my head in the clouds and the real world was just too hard to bear. That I needed careful handling. That I needed looking after.

Owen used to laugh when he heard that. He said that I was stronger than I looked. Steel wrapped in sensible wool. He had understood me at such a basic, visceral level, and I wasn't sure Florence could.

She put down her glass. "Right. Let's get changed."

I followed her up to my room. There was still time to change my mind, I told myself, but I knew I wouldn't. Florence was right, I needed this, to prove to myself that Owen was truly gone and no amount of table tapping and ringing bells would bring him back.

The memories, always present, raced through me. Like a train, rolling backwards, from this moment to the first time I met him.

FOUR

September 1915,
Belsham, Cambridgeshire

"What time is it?"

My father appeared in the kitchen doorway. I looked up from my crouch before the oven, strands of hair sticking to my face as I pushed the casserole back in for another half an hour.

"Lunch will be late. Why?"

"He said he'd be here around midday, but it's after that. I told him he could stay over at the pub if necessary."

I straightened and wiped my hands on my apron. My father and I often had these sorts of conversations, and I could usually untangle the meaning at the heart of them. Today I was completely confused.

"Who's coming at midday? What are you talking about?"

He stared out of the window above the sink, which was narrow and gave a view of the side of the cottage. The honeysuckle that climbed up the wall had begun to take over, so the tendrils were starting to cover the glass. I had taken the shears to it when I got up this morning, one of the reasons my hair was a mess.

"Owen Flett."

"Owen Flett?" I repeated, but my father had already turned and left. I heard his footsteps heading down the hall. I followed him, calling out. "Owen Flett, the journalist? The one you have been writing to forever?"

His voice drifted back to me. "Hardly forever, Emilia."

Owen Flett was a fan of my father's books and had written to tell him so. They had been corresponding ever since, and the connection had developed into a firm friendship.

Owen was one of the better known Fleet Street journalists, writing for the *London Courier*. I knew because I read all of his pieces. He seemed like a sensible man in an increasingly senseless world. I imagined him as a slightly younger version of my father, rumpled and distracted, his hair in need of a trim, the sort of man who had a tendency to stare into space, lost in his own head. And he was coming here for lunch!

"Why didn't you tell me?" Despite my moment of panic, I could at least congratulate myself on making plenty of casserole. I didn't always because it was wartime, and as such it was necessary to be frugal.

"I thought I did tell you," my father said vaguely as he pottered around the sitting room. He was the archetypal absent minded writer, while I was the one who dealt with life's practicalities.

Flustered, I went back to the kitchen, thinking about pudding. I could whip up something, as we had fresh cream from the farm down the road. I was already beating sugar into eggs when I heard voices, my father's and a deeper one, and stopped to listen. This had to be Mr Flett. He laughed, a sort of low chuckle, and it was the strangest thing, but the hairs on my arms rose.

"Emilia?" my father called.

I wiped my hands and quickly untied my apron. I wore an old woollen skirt that reached my ankles and a baggy sweater that had seen better days. Because of my honeysuckle adventure, my brown hair was coming out of the pins I had used to keep it up. We didn't get many visitors and I didn't feel presentable, but I told myself it didn't matter. Mr Flett was here for my father, not me. No doubt they would be locked away in his study for hours and my only task would be to supply the tea and food to fuel their conversation.

I stepped out into the hall with a smile and an apology for my appearance at the ready. He stood behind my father, and was quite a bit taller. The door was still open and for a moment he was a silhouette. Then he stepped forward and I saw him properly.

How to explain that moment? It wasn't so much that he was dark and handsome, although he was, and much younger than I had expected—early thirties, perhaps. It wasn't that his clothing was fashionable but understated, his Argyll sweater was pushed up to his elbows, and a soft leather briefcase was propped under his arm as if it lived there.

Perhaps it was his smile. His mouth curved up more on one side than the other, and his eyes coloured a light grey under thick eyebrows. Or maybe it was the way he seemed a bit shy, not at all the robustly confident sort of man I had expected him to be. But honestly, I think it was his presence. Everything seemed brighter and when he took my hand in his, a warm tingle ran down my arm and set up home in my chest.

"Miss Honeywell," he said, looking down at me. "The famous Emilia. I feel as if I know you. Your father dedicates all his books to you."

My father smiled, looking between us as if he had performed a magic trick. "Emilia tells me that lunch won't be long," he said. And then, leaning into his guest, added *sotto voce*, "She is a very good cook."

"My stomach is glad to hear it," Owen said, easily, charmingly, comfortably, as if we had all known each other for years. "Because I must say I am famished, Mr Honeywell."

"Call me Maurice. We know each other well enough to be on first name terms."

Owen smiled again. "I feel as if we do," he agreed, looking at me.

I remember standing in front of the mirror on my dressing table that night. Really looking at myself, in a way I hadn't since I was in my teens. Brown hair, unremarkable, brown eyes, equally so, skin that was clear and a smile that I supposed was sweet enough. I considered myself small but inclined to plumpness, although I was determined not to allow the plump to turn to fat. People said I was nice, that I was kind, and that it was a pity all the young men were away fighting and I wasn't likely to marry anytime soon.

Because that was what women were expected to do in Belsham. They married and kept house.

That I was looking at myself and thinking of Owen Flett was ridiculous. Perhaps I had inherited more of my father's imagination than I previously thought. Because now it had gone wildly romantic and very, very foolish. I threw an illusory bucket of cold water over myself. Owen would return to London tomorrow, and I would probably never see him again.

Earlier, over lunch, we had discussed the issues of the day, which mostly concerned the war. At one point I blurted out, "But won't the war be over by Christmas?" and he had given me a considering look.

"I fear that will not be the case," he said gently. "Do you have someone away fighting?"

"Quite a few of the boys from the village have joined up. I've lived here all my life."

"I meant a someone special."

I blushed. It was something I hadn't grown out of but was still hoping to. "No. No one like that."

He smiled, and I wondered if it could be interest I saw in his cool grey eyes. Interest with a hint of relief.

At supper he had spoken about one of the senior journalists at the *Courier* who had been chosen as a war correspondent. Owen thought the man was too old and set in his ways. I could tell that he believed he would do better.

"I have a feeling he won't be staying in the job very long," he added. "There's a rumour I'll be asked to fill in when that happens."

"When the time comes, you should take over," my father told him. "We need young, able journalists on the spot. We need to hear the truth and not the lies."

"Lies might be all I'm permitted to write," Owen said.

"How do you know unless you try?"

I remembered my father's words now as I looked in the mirror. How do you know unless you try? When had I ever tried to follow my own dreams? Suddenly, the cottage seemed too small for me, too restrictive. I was twenty-four years old and had lived in Belsham all my life.

I was my father's assistant, his appendage. I existed through him. His books took me to all parts of the world, in my imagination at least. But Owen's job had taken him to so many actual places! I had been fascinated as he spoke about Cairo and the pyramids. The Sphinx! Would I ever have the chance to experience such things for myself?

The next day, Owen came to see us before he left. He took my hand and looked down at me, thanking me for my excellent cooking. He promised my father he would write soon and wished him luck with his current book. We waved him off, and I'm sure we both felt the same way at his departure. We barely knew him and yet he had left a hole in our lives that would not be filled until we saw him again.

Owen had been right when he said the war wouldn't end by Christmas. It would not be over for a long time, if the stories seeping back from the front were true. I was sure Owen's were true, or at least as true as he was able to make them. He told me as much in his letters.

It was January now, and we'd been exchanging letters. At first, Owen had continued to write to my father, and he had starting asking about me—How was I? Had I made that delicious pudding again and could he have the recipe? Had I managed to tame the honeysuckle or had it taken over the entire cottage? Silly things that made me smile. One day my father said that I may as well write my replies directly to Owen, and that it would save him having to repeat the relevant paragraphs to me when he was a very busy man. But I detected a twinkle in his eye when he said it.

So I started writing to Owen myself. My first letter had been brief, despite having agonised over it for hours, and I almost changed my mind about sending it. I was even more anxious when his reply came.

Thank you for writing to me, Emilia. You don't know what a joy it was to hear your ordinary, everyday stories. You say you have nothing exciting to tell me. Never think that. I sift through so much grim news that your letter was a balm to my soul. I felt as if you had covered me in cream and treacle, and I smiled the whole day long.

I laughed. I had forgotten he could be silly. Sweet and silly. After that, I never found it difficult to write to him, and his replies were something I began to crave. Soon we were writing to each other regularly.

London is my home. As you know, I share a house in Easton Street with my younger sister, Florence. We rub along well enough, although she is a far more social creature. I hope to take a trip up to Belsham soon, if you will have me. Is your cottage as perfect as I remember it, and you and your father as warm and welcoming? Or did you put a spell on me?

And my reply: *As for the cottage, I'm not sure about 'warm'. Did you not notice the drafts that send a cold shiver down your spine when you sat in your chair at the dining table? Or the damp on the pantry wall? I'm glad you didn't notice because if you did, you may well change your mind about your visit. Please come. Father and I are longing to see you.*

He didn't come after all. The journalist who had been made war correspondent for the *London Courier* had fallen ill and Owen was asked to take his place. He had to pack and head across the Channel to the war. He apologised, and I shed some tears. I hoped he would stay safe. It was as if I already knew him, cared for him, in a way that seemed impossible.

FIVE

March 1919,
London

THE WORLD BEYOND Spiritualist Church turned out to be an upstairs flat above a bookshop on Tottenham Court Road. Florence and I entered from the street and climbed the narrow stairs, and were met by a young man standing on the handkerchief-sized landing at the top. When he asked our business, I handed him the flyer and after a cursory glance, he allowed us in.

We stepped into a sitting room with sofa and chairs, where about half a dozen people were already gathered. They looked at the pair of us with hungry eyes, or at least that was how it felt. I wondered if we were expected, but when they seemed to lose interest in us immediately, I realised we weren't who they had been waiting on.

A grey-haired man in a baggy three piece suit, eyes tired and his cheeks sunken, introduced himself as retired Major Goodrick and the woman beside him as his wife. She gave us a distracted nod, fidgeting with the glasses that dangled around her neck on a silver chain. The rest of the group ignored us, and I couldn't help but notice their frequent anxious glances toward the door we'd just come through.

"We're waiting on Miss Ward and Dr McIvor," the major explained. "Miss Ward is a medium." He frowned between me to Florence, his gaze lingering. Amongst this dull and sober crowd, my sister-in-law was an exotic bird. "Have you been here before? I don't remember…"

"No, it's our first time," Florence replied with her most charming smile.

"Are you seeking a message from a loved one?" Mrs Goodrick's blue eyes carried an intense stare. The lines of grief cut deep into her pale face. She twisted her glasses, glancing to the door again, as if unable to help herself.

"My brother," Florence murmured.

I realised then that I was no different to Mrs Goodrick and probably the others in this room. The worried eyes and tense shoulders. The low murmured conversations. Just like them, I desperately wanted to believe that Owen would come to me, that I would hear his voice and feel his touch. And frighteningly, despite my firm stand on the dubious nature of spiritualism, I would probably do just about anything to make it happen.

The sound of footsteps climbing the stairs brought the hum of voices to a halt. A plump cheeked woman appeared in the doorway, her mop of grey streaked hair speckled with rain. It was the same woman who'd sat beside me on the bus. I recognised her despite her lack of a face mask. Immediately the excitement in the room ratcheted up.

"Good evening," she said with a beaming smile as she removed her coat. Some of the others got to their feet and moved toward her as if they couldn't help themselves, at the same time responding to her greeting with their own.

"I do hope he will come to us today," Mrs Goodrick said, her eyes gleaming with excitement. The major gave her hand a comforting squeeze.

"Welcome to our gathering, good friends!" A male voice boomed from the door. Miss Ward wasn't alone. A man had stepped in behind her. He was of medium height, dressed in a three-piece suit that must have cost far more than Major Goodrick's. A well-trimmed beard followed the line of his jaw, and his dark eyes swept over the guests as though ticking them off in his head. He lingered a moment on Florence and myself, and then he smiled. Something about him fluttered a warning inside my chest—like a watchful bird stirring as danger slithered closer.

"I see we have some newcomers here tonight." He spoke loud enough for everyone to hear. "I am Dr McIvor. Welcome to you all."

He sounded friendly, and his smile was warm, but Florence leaned in close and whispered, "He looks like a magician. Do you think he will pull Owen out of a hat?" I stifled a laugh.

Miss Ward had also noticed us and smiled at me. Her curling hair was now drying in the warmth of the room, with untidy tendrils escaping the pins. Her round face was cordial, as if she had opened her arms to us, and I could understand why these people were drawn to her despite her unusual profession.

I didn't have time to speak to her, because now we were being herded by Dr McIvor through into another room. Here was a polished table, circular in shape, surrounded by chairs. Curtains were drawn over windows that might have looked down over the alley at the back, and the wooden floor creaked as we moved in a group across it.

"Take your seats, everyone," Dr McIvor gave the order in his cheerful way, but it was an order nevertheless, and we obeyed. Once seated, the scrape of chair legs against the floor loud in the hushed room, he turned to Miss Ward.

"We will begin shortly. Miss Ward? Are you ready?"

Miss Ward smiled and nodded, then settled herself more comfortably in her seat. Mrs Goodrick had taken a place beside the medium, with the major next to her. Florence and I were on the far side of the table, filling the last two chairs. I counted eight of us now, excluding Miss Ward. Dr McIvor stood slightly behind her, swarthy face serious and dark eyes intent. He didn't appear to be joining us.

"Will Jimmy come tonight, Miss Ward?" Mrs Goodrick asked, blue eyes fastened on the medium's face.

Pity tempered Miss Ward's smile. "You know I

cannot promise anything, my dear. I am only an outlet for the spirits; I don't call them. *They* come to *me*."

Dr McIvor spoke again in his commanding manner, rather like a ringmaster at a circus. Owen would have liked that. "Now, will everyone join hands, and this is very important for our newcomers—do not break contact. If you do, you will interrupt the circle and the spirits cannot draw upon our combined energy to make themselves heard. We will have to stop the séance."

Florence took my hand and, no doubt sensing my agitation, gave it a reassuring squeeze.

Once we were all holding hands, Miss Ward bowed her head and said a prayer. A nervous waiting silence followed. Dr McIvor moved silently around the room, checking for gaps in the curtains, and turning down the lamps. He left one on, over by the door, and by its faint glow I could see the shapes of the faces around me as well as Florence's newly dyed hair. There had been a fire in the nearby grate, but it had burned down so low it was now only a glow of atmospheric coals.

I wished I could have said there was a sense of 'something' in the room, but there wasn't. It was comfortable, almost peaceful, and the warmth made it increasingly difficult for me not to close my eyes and doze. My day had begun early, and I was ready for bed.

Time passed and all I could hear was Miss Ward's breathing as it grew deeper and slower. Her head began to nod, as if she too was falling asleep, until her chin reached her chest and remained there. Florence leaned in to say something to me, but she had barely said a word before she received frowns and glares from those nearby. Mrs Goodrick shook her head in approbation.

A draft came from somewhere. It stirred the curls that had escaped the medium's bun, as if someone was breathing on her. There were significant glances shared all around. Florence raised a sceptical eyebrow, but even she was not unaffected. The atmosphere had definitely changed. There was tension in the air, like a rope tightening. I felt as if something was about to snap.

Owen would have considered this all very theatrical. He had been deeply cynical about all such performances. A practical and pragmatic man. But he would have been entertained nonetheless. *"Oh Emilia, do you really expect me to appear in a white sheet?"*

And yet, if there was a veil between life and death, if he *was* waiting on the other side, then I longed for him to step through. I silently begged him to do so.

A sob came from somewhere on my left. The grief here was palpable. I understood these people. They were like me, longing for their loved one to return to them, if only for a moment of comfort. Such was life after the war to end all wars.

"Is Madge here?"

The voice made me jump. It was deep and gruff—a man's voice, but it had come from Miss Ward's throat.

"Madge, are you here tonight?"

"I'm here," a wavering reply came from the shadows on the other side of the table. "Frank? Is that you?"

"Madge," the voice went on gravely, "I want you to know that I'm all right. You mustn't worry. I want you to marry Michael. You deserve to be happy. I want you to be happy. Do not worry about me. I'm in a better place."

It was so strange to hear that voice coming from Miss Ward's throat that I couldn't help but stare. Her face seemed to be made of shadowy hollows, and it was possible to imagine the cheery woman from earlier had been replaced by someone else. Madge believed this was her Frank without even questioning it. But then, I reminded myself, these people had come here before, perhaps many times. They were members of the World Beyond church, and obviously firm believers.

Frank then spoke about everyday matters that Madge was familiar with, as if they were having a normal chat. After a few minutes, he wished her well and silence descended once more. Behind us, the dying embers were barely more than a spark and the sense of anticipation built until I could barely keep still.

Owen, please. Please…

"Hello? Polly?"

This time it was a Scot's voice, and he sounded loud and jolly.

"Oh, is that you, Douglas?" Dr McIvor stepped forward from his spot behind Miss Ward. "I'm sorry, but Polly isn't present tonight. I will let her know you were here."

Douglas didn't seem to be terribly worried and wanted to let everyone know that he was very happy and in a place where the whisky flowed like water. There were a few chuckles at that.

"There is someone new waiting to speak," he announced suddenly. "I'll give him the floor."

There was silence again.

Anna Ward seemed to have slipped lower in her chair, sinking deeper into her trance. Mrs Goodrick leaned eagerly toward her, her eyes unblinking. My gaze moved from face to face, and then to Dr McIvor. He was resting his hands on the medium's shoulders, and my eye was captured by some sort of mark on his wrist, where his cuff had risen up. The lamp light threw his features in sharp relief and I realised he was looking directly at me.

"He's here," he said with satisfaction.

"Emilia!"

The voice was so loud and frantic that my heart jumped violently in my chest. Someone gasped. Florence's hand tightened painfully on mine.

"Owen?" I croaked. Beside me, Florence was breathing audibly.

"Emilia. Don't … please … not safe."

Why did he sound like that? It was as if he was too far away, the distance making his sentence choppy. Like a wireless signal not quite tuned in to the station.

"Emilia! … Need to talk … to you!" He sounded agitated. I wanted to help him, I wanted to hold him.

I looked at Miss Ward while I listened to

Owen's voice, because it *was* his voice. Something strange was happening. It was as if Owen's features began to transpose on the medium's plump, amiable face. I leaned forward, my hands gripping Florence's and the woman on my other side.

Major Goodrick spoke in a harsh whisper. "Talk to him," he said. "Sometimes it is difficult for a spirit the first time."

"Owen?" Now it was Florence who spoke, and she sounded shaken. "Are you… did you suffer? When you…you died?"

I tried to tell myself it couldn't be real. None of it could be real. Owen was dead, and whatever was happening here was cruel and unkind. And yet this was Owen's voice, and I wanted to believe. So very much.

"Owen, is it really you?" I whispered. "Tell me something. Make me believe it's you."

There was a silence and I thought I'd scared him away, or else had somehow distracted Miss Ward. Disappointment grew bitter in my mouth. And then…

"Emilia," he blurted out. "The Remington. It's not a relic, for God's sake. Use it!"

I made a sound. A laugh or a sob, I wasn't certain. And that was when my last remaining doubts tipped over into total belief.

I tried to stand, but the hands on either side of me were pulling me back. My legs gave way and I fell back into my chair.

The Remington. Owen's beloved typewriter. It was old but in perfect condition, and I couldn't bear to use it even though my own machine was worn out. It was safely locked away in the spare room. How could Anna Ward know that I couldn't bear to use it? How did she know Owen owned a typewriter at all?

Miss Ward moaned softly and I heard Dr McIvor soothing her. Then she cleared her throat. "Mummy?" she lisped, and Mrs Goodrick began to sob.

The seance came to an end. The lamps were turned up, and the space was once again a normal room. Dr McIvor rubbed his hands together and asked everyone to stay for tea and biscuits. Miss Ward looked pale and drained, but she was smiling as she told everyone she hoped they had received messages from their loved ones. There were a few who hadn't, and she commiserated with them as she reminded them there was always next time.

I wanted to leave. Owen had spoken to me. I needed fresh air and silence so that I could think. I was confused and dizzy and felt rather sick.

The Remington. How would anyone else know about Owen's typewriter, hidden away, unused? I *had* turned it into a relic. He knew I needed a new typewriter. He was irritated I wasn't using his.

Mrs Goodrick had stopped weeping, although her smile was still shaky around the edges. She kept repeating how happy she was that her son had finally spoken to her. I hadn't even heard what he'd said because I had been so shaken.

"Here, drink this."

Florence stood in front of me, holding a cup and saucer. I took it from her but my hands were shaking so much that I had to put it down on the sideboard under the window. We were back in the sitting room with its cosy arrangement of furniture, where refreshments were being provided.

"Emilia?" Her grey eyes stared into mine, and I could see how knocked for six she was as well. "I don't want to believe it. I'm sure they could have found out Owen was a journalist. He's well known. He would have a typewriter, it stands to reason, but the brand? Could they have discovered that? Was it a guess?"

"He kept the Remington at home. He had a different one for work."

"Still, it's possible they found out somehow."

"I've kept it. I couldn't bear to use it." I rambled on, unable to help myself. "He would *want* me to use it, Florence. It's just what he'd say." I leaned close, my voice dropping. "He was here."

Florence shook her head, still playing devil's advocate. "How could he? He's dead. He died in Belgium. We know he's dead. The dead don't reach out from beyond the grave."

I could hear voices around me, happy voices mostly, although there were those who had been disappointed. Anna Ward sat in a comfortable armchair now, sipping from her cup as if the hot tea was the perfect restorative. Her plump face was gaunt and there were dark shadows under her blue eyes. She looked utterly drained and somehow diminished. Whatever had happened to her had taken a toll on her.

There was only one thing I could hang on to among the morass of doubt and questions, the hope that I could not seem to let go. I had heard Owen speak. He had come through the veil and I had looked into his face and heard his words. Owen had come back to me.

"We need to be careful," Florence's voice penetrated my elation. She took a nibble of her digestive biscuit and chewed thoughtfully. "It is easy to be drawn into these situations, Emilia. I've seen it happen to some of my friends. Their parents. Hope overrules common sense."

Too late. I was already sucked down into that place and I knew it would not let me go. How could I ignore Owen? For the first time since the telegram told me he was gone, I felt alive. Every part of me vibrated with life. It had been so long since I had felt this way. It was a shock to look about me and see how bright the flowers in the vase were, how vibrant the chintz covers were on the chairs. I hadn't realised how very drab my world had become until colour suddenly filled it.

"Mrs Flett."

Dr McIvor was had come to join us. Florence gave him a cool smile, and I felt her take a protective step towards me.

"I hope you were pleased with your first visit. I find people are often very sceptical until they actually experience a meeting for themselves."

I didn't know what to say. I felt tears in my eyes

and wanted to wipe them away, but it was too late. He had seen.

He gave me a moue of sympathy. "It is normal to be emotional." All the while he spoke, his dark eyes assessed me.

"Really?" Florence said. "I would never have guessed that chatting to your dead relatives could hurt."

He looked at her as one would a specimen in a jar. Then he smiled. "You are a sceptic. That is good. We will make it our mission to convince you."

Before Florence could answer, there was a cry. When we looked over to the group about the refreshments, I saw that Mrs Goodrick had collapsed. Already people fluttered around her, moving to her aid. Florence muttered something and hurried to join them.

I would have followed, but McIvor caught my arm and held me in place. Startled, I turned to look at him. This close, the mark on his wrist was clearer now. A tattoo of some sort. A face with greenery erupting from it—The Green Man?—and writing that looked like runes. He let me go.

"Mrs Flett?"

I directed my attention to his face.

"How long ago did your husband pass over?"

"Eighteen months." I felt the power of that dark gaze.

"A pity you did not come to us earlier. But never mind, you are here now." He smiled, but there was no kindness in it, only a sort of rapacious hunger.

I struggled to gather my thoughts. Did he mean if I had come earlier, I could have spoken to Owen earlier? That for the eighteen months I had been grieving, he had been waiting?

"I wonder if you would visit me tomorrow so that we could have a little chat? I think tonight has given you much to think about, but…" He bit his lip. "There is more we can do for you. So much more. Tonight, you heard your husband speak to you for the first time since he passed through the veil. What if I were to tell you that in special cases, we can arrange for you to see him face to face? To touch him in the flesh?"

"Touch him?" I breathed as if I had been running. I wanted to say no, shake my head. But he already knew I would like it more than anything in the world.

"Come here at noon tomorrow and we can talk. Privately." He let his gaze rest on Florence a moment. "Miss Ward will be here too," he added, as if that would ease any doubts. Then he let me go and immediately I stepped away. Something in his smug expression frightened me, and yet it drew me to him. He knew he was offering me the one thing I wanted above all else, and he knew I would be here at noon tomorrow.

By now Mrs Goodrick had been helped back into her chair. The woman was still pale, but her lips had regained some colour. My sister-in-law was too busy to have seen Dr McIvor talk to me, and for that I was glad. I didn't want to tell her what he had said.

I could have confessed on the way home in her

car, but I didn't. I kept it from her. I knew that was wrong, but I could not help myself. I didn't want her to offer me sensible advice, to warn me not to do it, to remind me how impossible it was for the dead to return, no matter how much we may wish it.

I wanted to believe Owen was waiting, and if there was a way for me to see him again, then I would take it.

SIX

I SLEPT LATE. I stumbled downstairs and found that Florence had left me a note to say she had an appointment to keep, but that there was food in the larder. She would be back in the afternoon. There was a postscript at the bottom.

You haven't met Eddie yet, so I'm inviting some friends around on Saturday and we are going to have a party. No arguing.

I was relieved she wasn't here, then I felt guilty because I was relieved. I knew I wasn't being honest with her. I was lying by omission because I wanted to hear what Dr McIvor had to say without her whispering doubts in my ear. I asked myself if I really believed that man could do what he had suggested? That I could see Owen face to face, that I could *touch* him?

I had always thought myself a sensible woman who knew such things were not possible. And yet I wanted to believe. I *wanted* it to be true.

When Owen was killed, we had expected to bring his body home, but no body had been found. We were told the trench had caved in, taking the men down with it, deep into the cold

Belgium soil. Any attempts to retrieve the bodies, or what remained of them, had to be abandoned when more shells began to explode around them. The dead were less important than the living, so Owen was left where he lay.

There was a grave with a stone on it in a churchyard with Owen's name on it, but there was no one in it, just an empty space in our hearts. My father had tried to comfort me. My feelings, he said, were understandable, but I should remember that the Owen we had known and loved, would want us to live our lives without mourning him forever. *He is sailing on the River Styx.* He meant that as a comfort, but it was no comfort. I had always imagined that waterway between Earth and Hades to be a dark and dangerous place, and I did not want Owen on it. Owen should be somewhere bright and sunny.

But if Dr McIvor was right, then he wasn't in either of those places, was he? He was still here, in my world, invisible yet able to make himself heard. Last night, he had sounded frantic. Desperate. Owen needed something from me, and I could not ignore that. I had to speak to him again and if that meant going alone to Tottenham Court Road, then I would do it.

I dressed and, after examining the timetable on the bus stop near the house, I set out.

London's streets were busy. People in influenza masks were everywhere, and the bus still smelt of damp wool and disinfectant. There was a service being held in a church and I heard the bell tolling as we passed. Then I saw a coffin being carried out to a hearse pulled by horses with sombre headdresses of black feathers.

People died, and their loved ones moved on. But how could I move on when Owen needed my help? Again, I remembered his words and felt my skin prickle. No, I couldn't abandon him when he needed me. I couldn't let him down.

It was already midday when I reached my destination. The bookshop was open today, and I could see several people browsing behind the windows. A table was set out on the street and the covers of marked down paperbacks flapped forlornly. I shivered as a chill breeze swept around the corner.

The street door was open, and I ascended the narrow stairs to the second floor.

In the weak daylight reflecting up from below, I noticed how everything looked rather seedy. The lamplight and shadows from last night had hidden the stains and a hole in the wall. Now I glanced about, feeling uneasy, but at the same time I wasn't going to turn tail.

Anna Ward opened the door almost immediately. She blinked as if surprised to see me. Then she looked behind her, into the room, before joining me on the landing, and forcing me to move back a step.

"Why are you here?" she asked, lowering her voice.

"Dr McIvor asked me to come."

"Ah." She smiled, but it wasn't a real smile. There was something uneasy about it.

"Last night," I blurted out. "Owen was upset."

She nodded. "He's come to me several times in the past weeks, then on the bus he was all around you. Whatever he needs to say must have been important to him."

"But he… He only spoke of a typewriter. That doesn't seem so very important. Surely he wouldn't come to me just to discuss a typewriter?"

Her expression was sympathetic. "Communicating with the living requires the dead to learn new skills. When they first pass over, they are not strong enough to make themselves properly understood. You may think his message was unimportant, but to him, it was very important. Something he was desperate for you to hear. Something that was worrying him at the moment of his death."

"So, there was nothing more?" I insisted. "You don't feel him now?"

She chewed on her lip and stared at the floor. "No, he isn't here now." Her behaviour was strange. Was she straining to try and sense him, or was she lying?

Before I could ask, she spoke again in a rush.

"Go home, Mrs Flett. Your husband has delivered his message and now he is at peace. You must learn to live without him until your own life is done." She was about to re-enter the room, but I reached out to stop her, taking her hand in a firm grip.

"Miss Ward…"

"He doesn't want you here," she insisted. "He doesn't—"

"Anna?"

I felt her jump. The voice came from the room behind us. Her gaze fixed to mine, and again I felt that she was trying to warn me. She wanted me to leave, but I was more certain than ever that Owen needed me.

Footsteps came closer and Dr McIvor's voice rang out in that commanding manner. "Is that Mrs Flett?"

The door was tugged opened and there he was, dark hair slicked back, dark eyes watchful as they flicked between the two of us. In daylight he looked different, his face all angles, thin and sharp. I felt as if something about him was wrong, as if I needed to protect myself. Or was that simply my reaction to Miss Ward's cryptic words?

"You should be resting," McIvor said in his forceful tone. He placed a hand on her shoulder and moved her gently but firmly aside, while she stared at him as if she was a fly and he was a toad.

Then he turned to me. "Miss Ward's powers are considerable, Mrs Flett. She was wasting them until I found her. Wasting them and wearing herself to the bone, which is why I believe it my duty to take good care of her. I make certain she rests often. You remember her stumble after last night's session?" He looked at the woman and raised an eyebrow.

Anna Ward forced a smile. "Very well, Dr McIvor," she said, "I will lie down for an hour."

"We have a private session later this afternoon. A member of the House of Lords, no less." He chuckled as if that amused him.

His gaze turned back to me. "Come in, Mrs Flett, so that we can talk. I will make some tea once Anna is settled."

It was odd. *They* were odd, but then I didn't know how people like this were supposed to behave. He followed Anna into a distant room and I heard the murmur of their voices as I turned and looked about me. The room felt different from last night. The comfortable overstuffed furniture seemed shabbier, and the air colder. Curtains had been pulled back and I could see the grey sky outside.

"She will sleep for a while." He was back without me hearing him. I turned too quickly, catching the windowsill to steady myself. He was silent now, watching me. His dark gaze took in my woollen coat with the fur collar and my scuffed boots. There wasn't a need for fashionable clothing in Belsham. My father certainly didn't notice what I wore. If anything, he dressed worse than I did. The thought made me sad, because for a time, after Owen and I were married, I had cared very much.

"My office is this way." Dr McIvor directed me to a room that overlooked a narrow laneway. There was a desk and a chair for visitors, as well as shelving, which contained numerous opaque glass jars.

"Why did you say that Miss Ward's talents were wasted?"

He gave me a curious look. "She was living with her mother and sister, entertaining their neighbours by calling spirits every Saturday night.

I was told of her by a friend and went to see. She is remarkable, and I told her so. I also told her that she could help so many more people if only she would allow me to help her. She agreed, and I persuaded her to join the church."

I was sure that Dr McIvor could be very persuasive.

He indicated the chair. "Sit down, please," he said in that same tone he had used with Anna. I wasn't sure I trusted it. I wished Florence was here and then reminded myself that I hadn't told her for good reason. My gaze next focussed on the glass jars. I thought there might be shapes in them, floating in some sort of solution.

"You asked me to come," I said. "Why?"

He stared at me a moment and gave a little laugh. The hairs on the back of my neck stood up. "You are disingenuous, Mrs Flett. You have spoken to your husband, but you wish to do more than speak to him. Now, don't protest, we both know it is the truth."

I bit my lip.

"You miss him very much, I think," he said gently.

And just like that, my pent up grief burst free. Tears ran down my cheeks, try as I might to hold them in. Nearly two years of loneliness and pain, two years without the man I loved and missed so desperately. I was done with being strong, of being stoic, of soldiering on. I wanted him back.

I felt the doctor's palm on my shoulder, then my face was pressed against his waistcoat. He smelt of earth—musty and yet not unpleasant, as if he had recently been gardening—with a faint undertone of bonfires.

"There, there," he said in a soft voice that seemed more satisfied than sympathetic. "I understand. You want your husband returned to you, and from what Anna has said, he is just as desperate to be with you. I can make that happen."

"That's impossible." I spat, lifting my head to stare up at him. He smiled, and I had that odd feeling again, as if my skin did not quite fit.

"Not impossible," he said. "I told you, Anna is a remarkable woman. It is unusual for a departed soul to return to the living, but your husband's situation is different. It can be done."

Dr McIvor smiled down at me, his face full of shadows, and I realised I wasn't just wary of him. I was *afraid* of him. Something inside me, an ancient part of my brain, was sending out a warning, but I refused to listen.

"I can have him back?" I whispered the words because I didn't think I could say them aloud.

You're being taken advantage of, Florence's voice cried out in my head. *They're going to ask you for money. Emilia, can't you see this is what all of this is about?*

I could see my white face reflected in his dark eyes. I looked tragic and yet hopeful. The perfect victim.

"Of course you can," he said. "For a price. Are you willing to pay that price, Mrs Flett?"

Disappointment smothered me like a cold wet blanket, damping down the flare of hope that had only just begun to spark. Florence was right, and I should have listened to her.

"A price?" I repeated stiffly. "You mean money?"

"Nothing so trivial," he answered with that easy smile. "And there will be time enough to talk of it after your husband is restored to you, Mrs Flett."

"I don't understand. You don't want payment first?"

He smiled. His incisors were sharp and his lips were red and moist, and suddenly I didn't want him touching me. I stood abruptly, almost knocking over my chair, and the words spilled from me.

"Tell me. What is the price for Owen?"

"There is no point in talking of price before the deed is done. Once you get what you want, then we will talk of payment, Mrs Flett. Not before. Surely that is more than fair? First, your husband returned and then payment? Believe me, when you see him for yourself, you will happily agree to my small request."

He knew what I had been thinking, of course he did. His mocking tone told me so. At the same time, he seemed very sure I would accede to his wishes. Well, of course he was. He was going to return my dead husband to me, make him live again. He knew I would do anything he asked if he could make that happen.

And the truth was I didn't care what he wanted from me. So long as Owen returned, what did anything matter? I felt quite light-headed right then, a little insane, and wild with hope and need.

"Before we proceed, Mrs Flett, I must ask you," he went on. "Are you sure?"

It seemed a ridiculous question to ask, but I forced myself to pause. To think. "He's been dead for eighteen months," I said. "His body…"

He waved a dismissive hand. "The body has nothing to do with it. The soul, the spirit, is what we are dealing with." He glanced toward the jars on the shelves. "One can dissect a hundred bodies and still the soul remains elusive. My studies over the years have taught me much, and I have found that once I have the soul, the ability of the body to regenerate is remarkable. Where there is a will and so on. The flesh is only part of what makes us who we are."

I hardly heard him. "Then I am sure," I said in a jerky voice. "Yes."

"Then it shall be done," he said with a note of satisfaction.

"I …" I looked around me. "Can I have him now?" I asked.

He laughed in that same mocking note, although there was pity in his eyes. "I only wish you could, but it doesn't work like that. *He* will come to *you*."

"But… when?"

"Soon."

"But…"

"A word of caution, Mrs Flett. Do not speak of this matter to anyone. I'm sure you understand why. And when your husband does return, he may not be quite as he was. He may have forgotten things or struggle to remember. That is as it should be. The shock of death, you understand. In time, he will recover his memory, or at least most of it. He has been through a truly terrible time and you must be gentle with him."

His hand was on my arm now and he was leading me toward the door. I was barely aware of what was happening, still overwhelmed, and then we were outside on the landing.

I opened my mouth to ask more questions, but he shook his head to stop me. "Soon," he repeated, and squeezed my arm through my coat. And the door closed gently in my face.

I didn't remember getting home, although I must have acted in a reasonably sane manner. When Florence returned, I was sitting in my room, which had once been Owen's. Some of his boyhood belongings were still there. I held a toy soldier, which he had painted meticulously in the colours of Wellington's brigade. Everything done properly. Everything in its place. Owen had always been meticulous. I wondered whether he still was. And then I remembered that soon I would be able to ask him myself.

Florence stood in the doorway, watching me. "Are you all right?"

"Yes. Well, you know." I wanted to tell her the truth, but I didn't dare. When Owen came home, then I would. Then she would see how right I had been.

"Come on," she said in a rough voice that hid her own emotions. "Forget about last night. I grant you it was all very odd, but we don't have to think about it now. Those people... they'll do anything to draw you in, Emilia. They probably found out about Owen's typewriter once they knew who you were."

"But they didn't know who I was. I met Miss Ward on the bus and I didn't tell her my name. They only learned it after I arrived."

Florence gave an uncomfortable shrug. "Well, they found out somehow. Let's change our clothes and I'll pour you a brandy. You look as though you need one. We can have some cheese and biscuits. I don't know about you, but I'm done in. Glad the party isn't until Saturday."

The party. Of course. I had forgotten about it. Would Owen be here by then? How long would I have to wait?

I still wanted to tell her that Owen was coming back, but what if she was right, and it was all lies? It wouldn't surprise me in the least if Dr McIvor enjoyed breaking widow's hearts. I looked up and saw that Florence was still there, in the doorway, and I could see the questions in her eyes.

I stood up. "All right," I said. "Give me a minute to change and I'll come down."

"You'll see," she said, relieved. "A party is just what we need."

When she'd gone, I turned to the closet. What on earth was I going to wear? The green silk dress was hanging inside. I had left it there when I went home to Belsham. I knew why. Owen had loved to see me wear it. The memories were just too strong and painful. Owen kissing my shoulders, lifting my hair so that he could breathe against my skin. His strong fingers undoing the fastenings…

I would wear it Saturday. I told myself it was in his memory, but a shaky, trembling feeling inside me said otherwise.

Soon.

SEVEN

THE PARTY WAS in full swing.

Florence's friends ran the full spectrum of London society, from the wealthy and privileged to the porter who worked at the hospital where she volunteered.

I had always admired that about her and Owen. They didn't care whether someone was a peer of the realm or a rat-catcher. Owen had told me once that he had felt the weight of his luck on his shoulders when he was young and had tried to find a way to ease the burden. He had an altruistic need to serve, to give back, and Florence had followed his lead.

Florence stood by the fireplace, a cigarette in a black ebony holder in one hand and a cocktail in the other. Her auburn hair glowed in the electric light above her as her companion—an attractive man with a moustache—leaned into her. She threw back her head and let out her husky laugh. Alexander's Ragtime Band played on the wireless, and a number of people were dancing with more enthusiasm than skill. There was nothing sedate about life after the war with these people. They were all out for a good time.

To give myself something to do, I had begun to tidy up the remains of our supper, until Florence told me there was no need, as she had someone coming in the morning to deal with the mess.

"Go on. Enjoy yourself," she scolded. "I insist."

I tried to. I really did. But I felt like an imposter, despite my bright dress. The green silk clung to my curves and my hair fell in curls over my back and shoulders, longer than it had ever been. Florence had attached a sparkly comb above my ear, and fussed over my lipstick and eyeliner. I looked glamorous as I sipped my gin and tonic and nibbled on my pate, but I did not feel it.

I spoke to those guests I knew, and those I didn't. I tried not to feel overwhelmed by the smells of cigarette smoke and booze and perfume. And all the while, at the back of my mind, was McIvor and what he had said to me. The look in his eyes.

I knew it was ridiculous to believe him, but I was my father's daughter, my creative brain ready to write my own story, make my own ending. Why shouldn't I have Owen back? Why wasn't such a thing possible if I wanted it badly enough?

On the other hand, believing he would come back was dangerous. This was England in 1919, not the Mount Olympus of ancient Greece. Dr McIvor wasn't Zeus, and the myth of Orpheus and Eurydice was just that. When Owen didn't arrive at my door, I was going to come crashing down all over again. I felt as if I was on the edge of a precipice, about to jump.

You are going to be destroyed, some sane part of my brain said. *How will you pull yourself up from this?*

My lips wobbled and I bit them before anyone noticed. Of course, Florence chose that moment to put her arm about my waist. She looked thin and elegant in her beaded white dress, while her hair was held back by a black velvet ribbon with a feather waving above it.

"Are you all right?" she whispered.

"Not really. I think I'll go up to bed."

"You can't! I need you here, Emilia!"

"You have half of London here," I reminded her with a reluctant laugh. "You don't need me."

"Darling, I miss him too."

I felt guilty then. Selfish. I had been thinking of my own grief, and I knew Florence missed her brother a great deal. They had always been so close, especially after their parents were gone. She had depended on Owen to help her navigate her way through her messy life.

Once again, I was ready to confess to her what I had done, until I reminded myself of the consequences. The pity in her eyes, the disbelief, followed by a hearty dose of chastisement.

"Sometimes I just need to forget," I said bleakly.

She waved an unsteady hand at the mass of bodies around us, the music suddenly elevated in volume as another jazz song came on. Since the war had ended, there seemed to be a desperate need for people to live life to the fullest. A wild, almost self-destructive air. Florence had chosen this way of life while I had locked myself away in Belsham, quarantining myself from everything that might remind me that Owen was gone.

"I know," Florence said, brightening. "Come and talk to Eddie. He'll cheer you up!" My sister-in-law tugged me towards a group by the drinks trolley. There had been serious inroads made into most of the bottles.

I learned that Eddie was a policeman, a detective inspector, which surprised me. Florence had always liked her men pretty and, as Owen put it, with boring jobs and deep pockets. Eddie was certainly handsome and well groomed, and his voice spoke of wealth and education, unusual in his chosen profession, but not unheard of. I often corresponded with retired policemen researching my father's books, and they were usually salt of the earth types. Eddie looked like an investment banker.

Someone bellowed that the champagne had run out, and Florence darted off to fetch more, with an apologetic glance at me.

Eddie gave me a smile. "Florence talks about you an awful lot," he said. I wondered if he was making an effort with me to curry favour with her. "I gathered you were close."

"As close as we can be, I suppose. This is my first time in London for a while."

I asked him how they had met, and he said it was at St Thomas's, the hospital where Florence worked. "I was there to interview a man who had been assaulted, and she was there to help the sick. As soon as I saw her, I knew I was going to ask her out, and no one was more surprised than me when she said yes."

"I can see why. You're not…"

"Her usual type?" he finished for me to my embarrassment. "So I've been told."

"I wasn't Owen's type either," I said quickly. To my dismay, my lips wobbled.

Something changed in his expression. Sympathy and kindness. It was always the kindness that undid me. Quickly I asked him about his work.

He quirked his eyebrows as if the question amused him. "As long as you don't want to talk about my most gruesome cases for your father's research," he said. "That seems to be what Florence's friends always want to hear. I'm afraid I deal with the uninteresting side of policing. Mostly racketeering and black market."

Shortages were still a problem, and I was aware that there were profits to be made by the unscrupulous.

As he spoke, I tried not to stare at a couple on the sofa, locked in each other's arms. The man had his hand on the woman's thigh, her hem pushed up, her red lips devouring his mouth.

Owen and I had been more discrete than that, but there had been times when our eyes had met at one of Florence's parties, everything in the room had gone quiet, and it had been only us. Once he had kissed me desperately at the station in Belsham and attracted the ire of a couple of elderly ladies, who considered public displays of affection scandalous.

We had giggled about it afterwards.

Eddie had said something, but I hadn't heard him. "I beg your pardon?"

"I said it's hard to get decent booze these days." He nodded toward the fast emptying bottles. "If I was wearing my policeman's hat, I'm sure I could ask a few awkward questions. The French brandy, for instance."

"Probably not the best way to ingratiate yourself with Florence's friends," I suggested.

He laughed. I was glad he knew when to take off that policeman's hat.

Someone was knocking on the door. It was loud enough that I could hear it above the party, and I looked around for Florence, expecting her to answer it as she had been all night. She was nowhere in sight, so I set down my gin and moved to answer it.

Eddie followed me. He seemed to have attached himself to me, and I wasn't sure what that meant. I suspected it was because we were both outsiders, fish out of water at this gathering. He was talking about a visit to the cinema tomorrow night. "Florence would love for you to come with us," he said. "She suggested I invite you."

I wasn't sure whether to feel touched or insulted. "What's showing?"

"*Tarzan of the Apes.*"

I laughed aloud. By now, I had reached the door and closed my hand on the catch, ready to turn it.

"My brother was killed on the Somme," Eddie said abruptly. "I miss him, of course, but life goes on. There's nothing we can do to stop it. I don't know if this helps, but I often tell myself that I need to live my life twice as hard. Live it for him and for me."

I liked him then, even more than I had before. He was genuine, honest, and he cared about Florence. He was a good man, but I couldn't help but wonder if that would be enough for her.

I might have said I was sorry about his brother. I might have said living life for the dead as well as the living wasn't always easy, or even possible. Sometimes just living was difficult enough. I didn't get to say those things though, because another knock sounded on the door, louder and impatient.

I flung open the door expecting to see another of Florence's well-heeled guests holding a bottle of black market booze.

There was no one there.

The street light outside flickered as if it was faulty, and the front steps were empty. Had they given up and gone away?

I was about to shut the door when a large shadow moved from the side, making me gasp. A figure stepped in front of me, and, too startled to move, my head jerked as I looked into his face.

It took shape, as if forming from the monochrome colours of the night. Familiar plains and hollows, the lick of dark hair that would never lay flat against his temple. I must have stepped back because suddenly the light from inside the house shone past me, bathing him in its warm glow.

Owen.

I meant to say it aloud, but the name stuck in my mouth, and I began to shake. My husband was there, standing in front of me as if he hadn't been dead for eighteen months. He even wore the same uniform. His grey eyes met mine, and there was a glitter in them, a flare of light. And then he said in the voice I had dreamed of hearing again for so long...

"Aren't you going to let me inside, Emilia?"

That was when it all became real.

I fell into his arms, stumbling against him, almost knocking us both over. It had to be a dream, but it wasn't. He was here. He was solid, warm flesh beneath the scratchy material of his jacket. I pressed my hands to his chest and ran them over his shoulders, searching for the injuries that had ended his life in the explosion. My fingers caught on something around his neck, a metal disc, and he took my hands in his, holding them tight.

With a sob, I pressed my face against him. He smelt of earth, with a note of charcoal, and somewhere in the back of my mind, I recognised it. But there was no time to think of that. I was overwhelmed, overcome, body and mind on the point of collapse.

Owen was here. He had come home. He had come back from the dead, just as I had been promised. I couldn't quite grasp it, the reality still too slippery to hang on to.

Somewhere in the background, I could hear Eddie calling for Florence. The next moment she was there, shrieking, and had her arms wrapped around us, so tight that it physically hurt.

"Owen, Owen!" she cried out.

Soon, everyone was there, crowding around us, until there wasn't enough air for me to breathe.

EIGHT

EYELINER RAN IN black stripes down Florence's cheeks and her eyes were red and puffy, but her smile was bright enough to light up the room. I sat on the sofa with Owen beside me, his arm tight around my shoulders, my body pressed to his side and my face buried in his chest. His body was so warm beneath the scratchy uniform, his voice rumbled beneath my cheek, and his heart beat in a steady rhythm.

He was *alive*.

"One of those war office blunders," he explained while everyone stared at him as if he was a ghost. "The trench I was standing in was blown to bits, but I was thrown into the officers' dugout and knocked unconscious. I don't know how long I lay there, but by the time I came around, the Germans had overrun our position, and I was a prisoner in a German hospital."

Someone murmured their amazement, but mostly there was silence. He had us all in the palm of his hand.

"There was a great deal of confusion, and then they were retreating and didn't have time to worry about me. Luckily, I was beginning to recover enough to keep up, although my memories were still hazy. Once I was able to, I escaped.

"There were so many refugees on the roads. It was impossible for the authorities to keep track of everybody. Eventually, I found a British camp, explained to them what had happened, and they were supposed to get word to you. That was eighteen months ago, and I thought they had. I didn't realise how my return from the dead would be received."

He glanced down at me and smoothed a finger over my cheek, and I was taking in every detail of him I could. There was something encircling his wrist. A scar? He saw me looking.

He grinned with a shrug. "A memento from the war."

"No one said anything to us." Florence was gazing at him in wonder. She kept reaching out and touching him, which made him smile. "We thought you were dead." Her voice caught on the last word. "We buried you, Owen!"

"I'm sorry."

"Don't you dare apologise for being alive!"

He laughed, and I snuggled closer to him. I hadn't said more than a word or two. I felt as if I just needed to assimilate the fact he was here, back with me. And as if he was aware of it, he kept leaning close to me, peering down into my face, brushing his fingers through my hair, like he did now.

"All right?" he asked me.

I tried to find my voice. He was here, he was *back*.

"You weren't dead," I said.

He shook his head, his grey eyes smiling down at me. "Never was. It was all a mistake."

Someone else asked a question, which he answered in a measured voice, but he looked as though he was enjoying being the centre of attention, even revelling in it. Which wasn't exactly an Owen thing—he preferred to duck out of the limelight when he could. Had the shock of the shelling changed him in some fundamental way? Or was it just that after so long away, with so much to tell, he might be enjoying his moment of glory.

For a moment, I was back in that room above the bookshop in Tottenham Court Road, with Owen's voice coming through Anna Ward's throat. Owen had been there, in the room with us, and yet that could not have been. Not if he had survived all along.

It finally dawned on me that I had been fooled. Perhaps Dr McIvor had already known that Owen was alive and on his way home, and had taken advantage of it?

The confusing thing was he had asked for nothing. Not then. The payment, whatever it was, would be made *after* Owen returned to me. Yet how could he claim to be responsible for this? Would he claim mastery over time as well as life and death?

My brain scrambled to make sense of it all. I told myself it was a coincidence, it must be. A series of unrelated events. I wouldn't think any more about it. Not now. All that mattered was that Owen was back.

Florence pushed the last of the guests out of the door, including Eddie. I saw him murmuring something to her and her shaking her head as if they were disagreeing, but that didn't matter right now. I was lost in my own world. I watched her make up a plate of leftovers from the party, then she led us up to the guest bedroom at the back of the house, hugged us both tight, and closed the door.

The room was cold from disuse, and the light from the window was barely enough to pierce the gloom. I didn't care. It could have been the palace at Versailles and I still wouldn't have cared.

"Come here," Owen said, and held out his hand.

I took it, feeling his strong grasp, his warm skin. I shook with emotion, or perhaps shock, and he noticed. He pulled me into his arms and held me until the shaking stopped.

"I thought I'd lost you forever," I whispered.

His breath stirred my hair, his fingers caressed my nape and my trembling returned, but for an entirely different reason now. My senses were stirring, needs I had pushed aside for so long were beginning to wake.

So many things to say and yet I couldn't utter a single one of them. He bent his head and kissed me. His mouth, his taste, the rough scratch of his unshaven jaw, all so familiar and yet it had been so long that he could have been a stranger.

He stepped away, releasing me, and unbuttoned his jacket. I rested a hand on the iron base of the bed, feeling unsteady. He was down to his shirt now, and dragged it off over his head, not bothering with the buttons. There was a puckered pink scar on his chest I wanted to ask about, but then I was in his arms again, his mouth on mine, and I felt his fingers unfastening the back of my party dress.

The green silk had always been his favourite, but all he said was: "I'm glad you're not wearing black," his lips moving as he spoke into the kiss.

"I did, for a while," I admitted, as the soft cloth slid down my body and puddled at my feet. "Then I remembered how much you hated it. Besides, I didn't need black to mourn you, Owen." My voice trembled.

He didn't answer. His eyes were on my breasts and he seemed to be entranced with the sight. "Emilia, you are as beautiful as ever," he groaned. "I dreamt about you over and over again. But my dreams did not do you justice."

I ran my hand up his chest, over the scar, and curved it around his neck. I could feel the pulse in there, beating. Alive. Tears filled my eyes and then he was kissing me again. It was important that he be inside me, that we be joined together. We fell onto the bed and there was no gentleness, just a desperate need to find what we had thought lost forever. Pleasure spiralled, making me gasp and him groan, slipping away into frantic kisses.

Afterwards, I fell asleep in his arms.

I woke suddenly, my heart thumping. I was somewhere else, somewhere dark. There were sounds in that darkness. People I couldn't see. A train rocketed through the night, the carriages shaking, on a desperate journey to somewhere. Someone's fingers brushed over my face, tracing my lips. Insubstantial, fading.

My eyes snapped open. Owen? The bed beside me was empty and my heart began to thump in panic.

Was it all a dream after all?

I might have called out, but then I saw the shape of him seated at the bottom of the bed.

We had forgotten to pull the curtains and he was looking toward the window, his face illuminated by the street lamp outside. High cheekbones and firm lips, and the dark hollows of his eyes below the heavy brows. It was Owen, and yet the way he sat so still, hunched forward, lost in his own thoughts, made me suddenly afraid. Despite his features, Owen's features, there was nothing familiar about him at all. In my rising panic, I began to ask myself whether I had invited a stranger into my bed.

He must have heard the change in my breathing. He turned his head sharply and his gaze fell on me. The shadows were even deeper now. The memory of my dream returned, and fear fluttered around me.

Then he was smiling. He moved back down the bed to lie beside me, his smooth naked shoulder beneath my cheek, and the face that turned to me was once again familiar and beloved.

"Emilia," he said. "I've missed you so much. So much."

It was all right, I told myself as he kissed me. Owen was home again and everything was all right.

NINE

WHEN I THOUGHT Owen had died, I had moved out of our London house and returned to Belsham. Florence had taken up residence, making the place her own, and I wouldn't hear of my sister-in-law moving elsewhere now. This was her home too.

Their parents had been a fixture in the London social scene, their father a doctor with prestigious patients among the upper classes, and their mother the daughter of landed gentry. Money had never been a problem, but the Fletts had believed in repaying the world for their privilege. That was where Owen got his social conscience from, as did Florence.

This might be their home, but it was remarkably unpretentious, and had always been more of a family home than a statement of power or wealth. I had loved it from the moment Owen first brought me here, and suspected that was because every corner held a memory of him. I remembered the stories he told me, with that shy half smile of his, making me love him even more.

Before he left for the war one time, I remembered him sitting in the nook in the kitchen downstairs, his newspaper open, stockinged feet propped up on the stove, completely content. It was the warmest place in the house, he told me. If his hair was messy and his shirt needed changing, then what did it matter? He deserved not to care. His job was demanding and his life uncertain, and it only grew more so the longer we were married.

And yet today he seemed unable to settle.

He wasn't sitting in the nook today, despite the chill in the air. Instead, he was walking from room to room, trailing his fingers over the surfaces, lifting objects and examining them as if confirming they were real. It was understandable, I supposed. Maybe, like me, he was trying to convince himself that he was really home and it wasn't all a dream.

I needed to give him time to come to grips with it. We all needed time.

Earlier this morning, Florence had followed me into the kitchen while I made tea to take upstairs. Owen had still been sleeping, peaceful, his naked back pale in the light from the window. I had pulled on my gown and crept out softly, closing the door behind me.

"I still can't believe it," she'd said, staring at me.

"Neither can I. But he's here. He's back."

Florence looked pensive, and I had an uncomfortable feeling I knew exactly what she was going to say. I tried to head her off, beginning to talk about what we would do with the day ahead, but she broke through my words.

"Are you going to tell him about the seance?"

I looked at her. "Tell him what?"

"That he spoke to us through a medium," she said impatiently. "Well, that we *thought* it was him, and he was asking about his typewriter?"

"It was all bunkum," I said stiffly as I finished putting the cups on the tray.

"Of course it was," she agreed. "All nonsense. But… should we tell him? He might want to write a story about it, so that others won't be taken in. Not that we were," she added quickly, "but you know what I mean."

"Let's wait." Would he think *me* foolish for being taken in?

Because how was I going to tell Owen about the conversation I had had with Dr McIvor? *He said you would come back to me, and that there would be a price to pay. And here you are.*

I couldn't say that, of course. It was all a coincidence, but when I remembered that conversation, I had an uncomfortable feeling in the pit of my stomach, gnawing at me.

Florence nodded. "All right." She chewed on her lip for a moment. "I asked Eddie to look up Dr McIvor, just to see if he's even a doctor. Eddie couldn't find any mention of him in the criminal records, so there's that at least, but he couldn't find him anywhere else either. He's not a doctor of medicine, or theology, or anything else, for that matter."

I stared at her in dismay. "What did you tell him? Eddie, I mean"

"I made up some story about meeting him at a party." She pulled her wrap close about her, tightening the belt. It was beautiful, made of Japanese silk, with flowers and birds painted on it. Her auburn hair was unbrushed, and her face was scrubbed clean of makeup.

"There's more. Eddie *did* find a Dr McIvor in Edinburgh, but that was almost a hundred years ago. He was a surgeon, involved with body snatchers, if you can believe it. Surgeons used to buy fresh cadavers to dissect for their research, and they weren't too concerned about where they came from. He disappeared without being charged. Perhaps our McIvor is a relative?"

I remembered the odd conversation I'd had with Dr McIvor in his room, surrounded by jars and their floating contents, before dismissing the thought. "Where *is* Eddie?"

She shrugged a shoulder. "At work."

"He seems nice," I ventured.

She smiled. "He *is* nice. Don't get too fond of him, Emilia, he may not last. He's probably far too nice for me. You know I prefer bastards."

She always said that, but I hoped that this time it wasn't true.

Later, Florence went out to do some shopping, so that she could make us something suitably celebratory for dinner, and that was when I caught Owen wandering the house.

"I'm extremely fortunate," he said, turning to face me. I hadn't thought he knew I was there, trailing after him like a shadow, frightened to look away in case he vanished. His eyes met mine and there was a spark in them, a heat that found an echo in me. The heat between us built until it felt as if the atmosphere itself was combustible.

"Come back to bed," he said.

Florence had set the dining table with the good china and we sat together while she fussed about. Owen laughed at first, but as the meal went on, I noticed he seemed to get more irritable. I had always loved his calm demeanour, but now he seemed to have lost the ability to remain still.

I told myself changes were to be expected. Of course he would be different now. How could he not be? The last eighteen months had changed me as well.

"Remember Balfour?" Florence said, looking up with a smile, her eyes bright.

Owen chewed his food and frowned. "The Prime Minister?"

"No, our dog! The Scottish terrier. Father insisted on calling him Balfour because he … Anyway, do you remember when—" And then she was off, repeating stories from the past, never stopping for breath.

I imagined it was because she was still processing the wonder of having Owen back again, and she was trying to say all the things she had wanted to say over the past eighteen months. I understood that, but I wasn't sure Owen did.

He began to frown, the line between his brows deepening. I didn't remember it being that deep, that permanent. I imagined that his life as a prisoner and then a refugee had not been easy.

"You don't remember Cousin Sybil?" Florence was laughing. "Come on, she was so memorable! Let me find a photo of her in the album."

She got up, knocking over her wine glass in her haste, splashing the merlot from the crystal glasses she said had been her grandmother's. The red liquid went all over the white cloth, and splattered Owen's plate.

He jumped up, uttering a curse I had never heard him use before. We all froze. He was breathing hard, his chest rising and falling as if he'd been running, and his grey eyes were almost… feral.

"I don't remember *bloody* cousin Sybil," he said, his voice low and angry, vibrating in his throat. "I don't care about bloody Balfour the dog. Can we please just sit and eat our meal in peace?"

Florence stared at him in shock, still half out of her chair. Red continued to spread on the cloth in front of her.

Owen pushed his way out from the table and stalked off, slamming the door behind him. We could hear his footsteps up the stairs and then the slam of the bedroom door.

There was an uncomfortable silence, then Florence sat down again and put her head in her hands. She began to shake it back and forth, whispering to herself, "Stupid, stupid."

I came to her and rested a hand on her shoulder. She pushed her hair out of her eyes to look up at me and I could see they were bright with tears.

"Sorry," she said. "I pushed him too far, didn't I? I was just so …"

"I know."

"It's not like I don't know better," she went on, a wry twist to her lips. "I've seen men at the hospital who are struggling since returning home. Some of them are deeply affected, physically and mentally."

"He'll just need some time to himself," I reassured her. "Coming back here after everything he's been through, after being so sure he'd never come home. It must be—"

"Yes. Sorry. I'll try not to bombard him," she said, but there was pain in her eyes, and sadness. I wanted to tell her I knew how she felt. She wanted her brother back as he had been before, as did I, but I wasn't sure that was possible.

Florence looked at the mess on the table. She sighed. "I'd better clean this up."

"I'll help," I said, instead of what I was going to say.

By the time we were finished it was late. I refused Florence's offer of cocoa and made my way upstairs.

I cautiously opened the door, in case Owen was asleep, but he was sitting up in bed, bare chested, holding a cigarette. Owen never used to smoke, so he must have taken it up the way so many of the men at war had. It was yet another change in the man I had thought I knew so well.

He narrowed his eyes at me as he pulled on the cigarette between his lips. "Is she all right?" he asked quietly. "Florence?"

"She was sorry she upset you. She's just so pleased that you're home. She got overexcited."

He nodded and took a last drag on the cigarette before putting it out. I noticed he was using one of the saucers from the tea set in the glass case in the dining room. Probably worth a fortune, I thought, but didn't say anything. They belonged to his family, after all.

"Sometimes I need to …" He frowned, that line between his brows deepening. "I just have to have some peace and quiet." His voice grew ragged. "The *thump thump* of the guns gets in my head. The shells coming into the trenches and the ground shaking. Even behind the lines, I could hear it. It never went away. I longed for quiet."

"It's all right," I said, coming closer. I didn't want to touch him. He was trembling, his body shiny with sweat despite the chill in the room.

He glanced up with an apologetic look. "I'll apologise to her tomorrow," he said.

I nodded.

"I didn't even remember half of the things she was saying," he said, with a grimace. "The shell, I suppose, and what followed. It's left holes in my memory. I was embarrassed I couldn't remember the dog or Cynthia."

"Sybil," I corrected him before I thought better of it. "Doesn't matter," I went on quickly when he went still. "None of that matters. We're just so thankful you're here with us."

"Even if some of me is missing," he said, trying to make a joke of it, but I could see the doubt in his eyes.

"Even then."

I went to him, my arms around his waist, my face pressed to his chest. He stroked my back absently, and kissed the top of my head.

"Take your time," I said. I wanted to rub my face over him like a cat, luxuriating in his scent, but stopped myself. I could feel him tensing, as if at any moment he was going to get up and move away from me. He'd said he needed quiet and perhaps he needed to be solitary too.

"We have all the time in the world now you're back."

TEN

SINCE OWEN'S RETURN, I had been eager to tell my father the wonderful news. I should have done it already, but a week had flown by, and I suppose I'd been selfish. I knew I couldn't just turn up in Belsham with my dead husband in tow though. I needed to speak to dad on the telephone first and tell him of the miraculous news.

He'd be over the moon. He had always treated Owen like a son, and Owen had been his friend long before he was mine. Although he was in good health for his age, he was going to find it a shock. A good one, but a shock nonetheless.

"Emilia, is that you?" He came onto the phone, breathless, after I had almost given up. "Will you be home soon? That girl from the village has *dusted* in my study. Can you believe it? You know I never allow that! And she cooked me a fish pie with the bones still in it. Madness!"

"Oh dear. I am sorry. Yes, I'll be home tomorrow."

"What time does the train get in? I'll meet you."

"I'm not coming by train." Owen was going to drive me. "Dad, there's something I have to tell you. Something wonderful. I need you to be prepared."

There was a pause, and again I heard him breathing. "You've met another man." His voice sounded flat.

"No! No, I haven't. Dad, Owen isn't dead. It was all a mistake. He was a prisoner and … I'll explain everything when I see you. All that matters is that he's alive and he's come home. We'll be driving up to Belsham tomorrow." Now the pause was longer and he made a strange sound, as if he was trying not to cry.

"Owen is alive?"

"It was a mistake, Dad. There was a clerical error and they didn't tell us, and he-he came home. He's all right, just a little… well, he's been through the mill a bit. Dad? Are you there?"

Eventually, he came back on the line. His voice was unsteady and his breathing ragged, and he said he was happy, very happy, and he would talk to me tomorrow. Then he hung up.

I knew he would be crying, and needed time to assimilate what I had told him.

I put the receiver down and turned and jumped, because Owen was standing in the doorway. He had been listening to me and I smiled, wiping the tears from my cheeks. "Dad is so happy. You know how he feels about you."

He came and wrapped his arms around me. "I may not remember everything," he warned me, his breath warm in my hair.

"It's all right. He'll understand, and if he doesn't, I'll explain. You know how you always loved the village. You said the last time, when you left, that you would like to live there."

"Did I?" It wasn't quite a question. He sounded surprised.

"Not yet," I added quickly. "I don't mean now. You have your job in London, after all."

There had been no mention of his job since he came home. I had wondered if he had been in contact with the *Courier* or whether they had given him leave. Once I would have asked anything of Owen and expected him to answer, but everything had changed, and I found myself tiptoeing around him in a way I never did before.

"There is my job," was all he said.

I left it there. After Florence's dinner, I had made the decision not to push him. He would tell me things in his own time, when he was ready.

The car was safely tucked away in the garage in the mews at the back of the house. Florence and I had spoken about selling it—she had her own car—but the Daimler had belonged to her father and when he died, it had become Owen's. It was red, a two-door coupe, and his father had bought it in 1910, the year of his death.

A last gesture of rebellion, Owen had always said, for a staid and respectable Harley Street doctor. All his life, Mr Flett had been exactly that, staid and respectable, and it was only at the end that he had begun to show signs of wanting to break out of that box. Owen loved the car because it was his father's, but also because it had signalled to him that it was never too late to change.

Florence and I hadn't sold it, we couldn't bear to in the end, and so it had been safely tucked away.

Owen's face lit up when he saw it. Suddenly he was like a young boy, excited, touching the shiny red body and standing on the running board so he could peer into the interior of the Daimler.

"Florence says it's ready to go," I said, blinking away the tears that threatened to spill down my cheeks. Despite the fact they were happy tears, the new Owen didn't like me crying over him. I remembered the irritated glance he'd given me last time.

"I always wanted one of these," he said.

I laughed because it was a strange thing to say. He grinned at me over his shoulder. "Are we going now?"

I looked down at our cases on the ground behind me. "Yes, we're going now," I teased. "If you stop admiring your car and start it up."

His grey eyes clouded a little. "You might have to direct me. Some of the way at least," he added, when he saw the doubt in my face. It was difficult to hide my emotions from him. I had never been very good at it.

I tried to tease him about it. "You used to say you could drive there with your eyes closed."

His face turned sombre. "Sometimes there're gaps. There are times when it's as if my memories belong to someone else, and it's difficult to navi gate them. As if *I'm* someone else." He looked at me then, waiting to see what I would say.

"I'm sure you've noticed," he added when I said nothing. "I didn't want you to think I was being awkward. You mean everything to me, Emilia, and I'd hate for you to think I'm not the man I was."

I stretched up and kissed his cheek. He smelt of his familiar cologne and shaving cream, his coat smelt the same too, although it had hung in the closet all this time. He was Owen and I wanted to tell him that it didn't matter. None of that mattered, because I loved him.

Perhaps he knew that, or perhaps he didn't want to discuss it any longer, because he put an arm about my shoulders and squeezed, and a moment later he was loading the luggage into the dicky seat.

The suburbs of London were left behind and Cambridgeshire opened up before us, flat and windswept, the sky a grey canvas above us. I had rugged up warmly for the drive, but Owen didn't seem to notice the weather.

It was only 10 miles now to Belsham, and the roads had narrowed. Belsham was a small village, but in medieval times it had been an important trading town with an abbey. My father knew the history and had lived here all his life, apart from a brief fling with a place in Cambridge after he and my mother met and married.

He must miss her, in fact I knew he did, but he was content with his books and his quiet life. With me. He had never wanted anything more, and famous as he was, it meant no more to him than a means to continue living in Belsham and writing. His books were about places and people he would never visit or know, and I think he was more than happy with that.

We reached the beginning of the village, and it seemed as if Owen wasn't going to slow down. "Turn just up here," I said. I had been watching his face off and on as he drove, seeing the simple joy he felt to be out in his car. His gloved hands gripped the steering wheel in a manner that was so familiar, as was the way his shoulders filled out his favourite cashmere coat.

I'd been holding his hand when he wasn't busy driving. I liked to trace the scar that encircled his wrist. It resembled a twisted vine, so that was how I thought of it. I had asked him once where his injury had occurred, but he shrugged and said he didn't remember. As he slowed to make the turn, I put my hand on his thigh, just to feel the warm skin beneath the cloth of his trousers, just to have that contact with him.

He gave me a sly sideways look beneath his lashes. "Don't start something you can't finish," he said, almost in a growl.

It made me take my hand away. Owen and I had always had a strong physical connection, but he'd never spoken to me like that. He loved me, I never doubted it, but he was shy with women, even me. He was respectful, gentle, and just now he had been neither.

"I, uhm," I heard myself stumbling over my words. Would my shy, awkward husband have said something so loaded with sexual intent? I wondered what encounters he may have had while he was away, and whether there had been other women.

"The cottage is at the end here, isn't it?" he said, slowing down even more as we approached the end of the lane. Tall trees set a backdrop and I could see the whitewashed walls and the garden at the front, currently in hibernation, but in the summer it would be a glory of colour. I was home, and I was relieved on one hand while on the other I was anxious, because Owen and my father were about to meet again. I shouldn't be anxious. I didn't really understand why I was. This was going to be a happy occasion.

So why was I worried that it might go badly? Perhaps because when I had told him that my father expected us to stay for a few days, I had seen Owen's lips tighten. These days I was forever looking for signs that he wasn't pleased.

By the time we stopped outside the gate, my father was coming out of the door. He must have been watching out for us, which only went to show how happy and excited he was. He had felt Owen's loss keenly. Now I held my breath.

"Owen?" he said as he reached the car, his eyes shiny with tears.

Owen jumped over the side of the car, not bothering with the door, and clasped Dad to his larger frame.

"It really is you." My father's face had such an expression of joy on it, I found I was struggling with my own tears.

"It really is," Owen responded, and pulled away. He slapped my father on the back, startling us all. Perhaps it was a good thing though, I decided, because it broke the emotional moment. Made it more bearable.

"That *girl* cooked a casserole," Dad said, surreptitiously wiping his eyes. "I think it's burnt."

I smiled. "Never mind. I can make something else if it's unsalvageable. You and Owen can have a chat in the study before we eat," I added. "There must be so much for you to catch up on."

"I'm nearly finished my book," Dad said with the excitement he always had when he spoke to Owen about his writing. "I remember how much you were looking forward to reading it."

"You mean…?" Owen's voice trailed off.

"You remember? The one about the soldier who commits a crime in the heat of battle and then covers it up."

A strange expression clouded Owen's face.

Before Dad could carry on, a cold blast of air came across the fields on the other side of the lane, and Owen took my arm. "Let's get Emilia inside," he said. "She must be frozen."

As he walked me toward the open cottage door, I told myself he was being thoughtful, and I *was* frozen, but also that he wanted to change the subject. He'd forgotten about the book my father was so excited about and he was embarrassed. Should I warn Dad that Owen may not be quite the same as he was? But how could I do that without Owen knowing, or Dad becoming excessively cautious. I didn't want to spoil this moment between them.

It was better to let them find their own way around the difficulties. They always had before.

In the kitchen, I found the casserole in the oven. It was very brown on top but not inedible after all, and there were vegetables cut and ready to steam in the pot on the hob. I could hear murmured voices in the sitting room, and smiled to myself. It was all so normal, as if nothing had changed, but I would never take normality for granted again. At least, I hoped not. I hoped I would never take Owen being by my side for granted either.

I found eggs and flour and butter and whipped up a sponge to go over some stewed fruit. There was cream too. The girl from the village, despite my father's complaints, seemed to have managed very well. I stood a moment, wondering what would happen now that Owen was back. Would we stay here awhile? Would I come home and he remain in London, until domestic matters were sorted out? I didn't want to do that. I didn't want to leave him for a moment and I wasn't ready to admit to myself why.

Once the meal was ready to serve, I went to tell them. When I reached the doorway into the sitting room, I found to my surprise that the two of them were no longer deep in discussion. Dad was sitting, hands folded over his rounded stomach, looking at Owen in a worried, watchful way, and Owen was staring out of the window as if he wanted to escape.

"Lunch is ready," I said quietly. They both turned to me with obvious relief.

Owen moved to the door. "I'll just have a cigarette first."

Dad had begun to stand up too, but paused halfway to stare. "You smoke now?"

Owen grimaced. "I know. Filthy habit. But I got used to it over there and somehow... Well, it helps to calm my nerves."

Dad's expression of distaste turned to sympathy. Realising I was watching him, he forced a smile. "How was the casserole?"

"I think it's fine. Dad, now that Owen is back—"

Maybe he knew what I was going to say and preferred to discuss it in private because he interrupted me. "Let me help you with the plates," he said, which was surprising in itself. My father was rarely thoughtful when it came to domestic matters.

"What did Owen think of your book?" I asked once we were in the kitchen, partly for something to say, and because I was curious.

"He didn't really feel up to reading it." He was behind me, so I couldn't see his face, but I heard the tone in his voice. Disappointment.

"Florence said that she sees a lot of men who have come home from the war changed and it takes time for them to recover." I didn't add that sometimes those men never recovered. "Owen just needs time, Dad."

"I know that," he said impatiently. "It's not that. I'm just…" But whatever he was going to say, he changed his mind. "Has he spoken about what happened to him over there?"

"A little. I'm letting him tell me in his own time."

"Good, good."

"I do notice changes. He's different."

"Yes, he is."

I considered telling him about the seance. It would be a relief to tell someone, and I knew my father would listen to me even if he would shake his head at my foolishness. I had behaved like a gullible and desperate woman, rather than the sensible and level-headed daughter he believed me to be. But now he seemed far too distracted and instead of reassuring me, I was worried he would lecture me on my silly behaviour. I didn't need a lecture, not now, when we were about to sit down to our first meal together after so long apart. The two men I loved most in all the world.

When Owen came back inside, he said the right things—how hungry he was and how good it smelt—but we ate mostly in silence. I tried to tell myself that it was a good thing because it meant we were all comfortable with each other, but that wasn't true. There were so many things to discuss and yet I felt I couldn't.

After the meal was finished, Owen went outside for another cigarette, and I told my father to go sit in the other room while I tidied up. By the time I brought in the teapot they were both in there. My father's eyes were closed and he was dozing in front of the fire. Owen was standing up, leaning against the mantelpiece, staring at some of the antique shepherdesses that my mother had collected. He slipped his hand into his pocket and turned to me with a smile.

"Thank you," he said, taking the cup I handed to him and then not seeming to know what to do with it. He only took a couple of sips before he set it down. "It's been a long day," he told me, pulling a face. "Too much fresh air. I'm going up to bed."

"Do you remember the way?" I asked, ready to show him, but he gave me that irritable look and said of course he did.

I stayed a little longer, putting away the bits and pieces my father had put down and then forgotten, setting up the fire guard. Dad would probably sleep for a while and then do some work, so I left him and climbed the stairs to the bedroom. It was dark, but the curtains were open to the night and a few stars had found their way between the clouds. I noticed that Owen preferred to leave the windows bare in our bedroom. I undressed hastily in the chill, and after a quick wash in the basin, climbed into bed beside my husband.

In the past, I would have cuddled up against his side, or at least found his hand and linked my fingers in his. Now I lay in the darkness and listened to his steady breathing, the occasional soft snore. I could feel his warmth even though we weren't pressed together, and it comforted me. After a moment, I did reach out and find his hand, and his fingers tensed around mine, and then relaxed again.

I told myself everything was all right, and we would make our way through the difficulties this new world had thrown in our way. Our relationship might not be the same as it used to be, but we could rebuild it. Owen was home and safe and alive, and that was all that mattered.

The sound of a shotgun woke me up. After a moment of confused shock, I realised it was the farmer on the other side of the lane. Mr Stewart. He shot at the crows on his property and despite my father's lengthy complaints, he wouldn't stop, and now he was at it again.

There came another shot, and another, the sound echoing loudly, shattering the peaceful morning.

Between shots, I heard another sound. Sitting up, I realised Owen wasn't there. Then I saw him, crouched beneath the windowsill, hands wrapped around his head.

"Owen?"

He was half naked and shaking. Quickly, I went to him and held him tight, feeling his chest rise and fall with each ragged breath, before he buried his face against me.

"Make them stop. Make them stop." He said over and over, an anguished groan interspersed with gasps for air.

I murmured comforting words, so intent on making him better that I didn't realise that his mantra had changed.

"I don't want to die. Make them stop. I didn't mean to do it. I couldn't help it. Couldn't help it. Couldn't…"

I held him until the farmer went away, taking his shotgun with him. I held him until he stopped shaking and his breathing returned to normal, and then, as if embarrassed, he shifted back. He ran a hand through his hair and stood, avoiding my eyes.

"Owen?" I stared up at him, stiff from my uncomfortable position—the cold seemed to have seeped into my bones.

I wanted him to talk to me. The shotgun must have brought back memories of the war, memories that he wanted to keep locked away. He seemed ashamed by his reaction, embarrassed, and I wanted to reassure him that I understood and it didn't matter.

"I'm going down for a cigarette," he said, still not looking at me. He reached for his clothes, quickly pulling them on, then walked to the door. He opened it and closed it gently behind him.

I leaned back against the wall and stared at nothing. I didn't know what to do. I wanted to help him, but didn't know how. I needed to talk to Florence again, talk to her about patients of hers that had behaved similarly to Owen, try to come up with a plan. I told myself there was hope if I was willing to seek it out. But at the same time, I knew that Owen was the only person who could explain to me the memories twisting in his poor, tormented brain.

I didn't mean to do it.

What terrible things had happened to my husband in the eighteen months I thought him dead?

ELEVEN

DAD WANTED US to stay longer, but Owen declined the offer rather brusquely, saying he needed to get back to London and that his editor was expecting him. I knew my father was hurt but I couldn't insist we stay, not after what had happened this morning. Mr Stewart sometimes fired at the crows several days in a row until he had driven them off. Owen's suffering was not something I could prolong.

I hugged my father and sat in the car, where Owen was already in the driver's seat. His goodbyes had been perfunctory, as if he was eager to get moving, and while I understood it, it made me sad. Sad for my father and sad for Owen.

Give them time, I told myself. They'll find each other again.

Things will get better.

On the drive back, we stopped at a pub and sat at a garden table in a patch of sunlight while the world moved at a slow pace around us. We hadn't spoken much, but I could tell that Owen was much recovered from earlier, eagerly ordering food and a drink, smiling at me when I pointed out some children playing by a duck pond.

"How often did we used to visit your father?" he asked.

"Well, you know Dad is on his own. You and he always got along so well."

"How often?" he repeated, a stubborn set to his mouth.

I tried to hide my surprise and disappointment, but he wasn't looking at me. He was staring down at the table, picking a broken piece of wood with one finger.

"I can always go down by train," I said at last, making my tone light. "You don't need to come. Especially if you're working at the newspaper. You said Sir Richard wanted to see you?" Sir Richard Laurens was the owner of the *Courier*.

I was glad to see his face relax, and when he smiled I knew I had done the right thing. He reached to take my hand affectionately in his.

"When do you have to go into the newspaper?" I asked when he didn't answer my question. "I suppose they'll want you to start work again soon?" I heard the anxiety in my voice and stopped, realising how carefully I was treading. I don't want to upset him, that's all, I told myself. Nothing wrong with that, surely? He's suffered and I am trying to protect him.

"Why? Do you want to get rid of me?"

I laughed, thinking he was making a ridiculous joke, but then I noticed the suspicion in his eyes. "*Why?* Because that's your job. I expect they'll put you on the front page. You are a bit of a miracle, after all."

I smiled brightly, but again I saw the hint of wariness in his expression.

"Never mind," I said quickly.

"No, you're right." His mouth firmed as though he were stepping up to the mark. "I need to go in and talk to Sir Richard. I'm being a coward. It's just …" Now he gave me his lopsided smile, his 'Owen' smile. "I wanted to spend more time with my wife."

My heart melted. It was moments like this that buoyed me up in the dreadful sea of concerns I sometimes found myself drowning in. That one smile reminded me that Owen was still in there, waiting for me.

One of the children by the pond waved to us enthusiastically and I waved back. Owen and I had spoken of children before, of wanting them when the world was a safer place. I still wanted children, but I wondered if he still did. I almost asked him, but didn't. Another time, I told myself, and there was plenty of that now.

Before we left, I went into the pub's loo to tidy myself up. An open topped car was not the best thing when it came to keeping one's hair under control, and mine had been whipped into a bird's nest. Satisfied with the results, I made my way back to the garden.

Owen stood by our table, talking to the woman who had served us earlier. I remembered her chatting about the weather. The two of them were laughing, and then she leaned in close, her hand on his arm. My steps slowed. I wondered what they were saying that was so, well, intimate, but before I could reach them, they had broken apart. Next moment the woman came bustling toward me, still smiling.

"Hope you enjoyed your meal," she said as she passed me, and gave a meaningful wink. There was something so suggestive in her manner that I was taken aback.

"Yes, we did. Thank you."

She turned. "While the wife's away, eh?" she said with a chuckle, and vanished inside the building. I stood there, staring after her.

What did she mean by that? Did she believe Owen and I were on some sort of illicit getaway? Somehow, she had got hold of the wrong end of the stick. It was a little annoying, even though I tried to tell myself it didn't matter.

And yet… I felt as if the world had tilted to one side and I was sliding down some unseen chasm, scrambling to find purchase.

Owen had already started the car when I climbed in. "Ready?" he asked in a clipped voice. It was probably my fault, my own tardiness.

He used to open my door. The memory popped into my head. *He used to wait for me and then open my door before he went around to his side.*

Why was he so impatient to leave when only a moment ago he had been telling me how much he wanted to spend time with me? I didn't mean to be suspicious but I couldn't seem to help it. The words came out of my mouth before I could stop them.

"What were you talking about?"

He barely glanced at me. "Talking about?"

"You and that woman. What were you talking about?"

"Why? Are you jealous?" He asked it in a voice I could not remember ever hearing before. Sort of amused and sly, yet irritated. As if I was one of those nagging wives comedians joke about.

Before I could answer him, he said, "She was asking whether we had enjoyed our lunch, that was all."

"Then why did she think you were married to someone else?"

He barked out a laugh. "She *what*?"

"She made some remark about 'while the wife's away.' She thought you were married to someone else."

"I don't know, Emilia," he said, still grinning. "Perhaps you should take it as a compliment that she assumed you were the Other Woman." Then, when I didn't smile at his attempt at humour, "It was nothing. Forget it." The irritation was back.

He pulled out, making a wide circle to get back onto the road. I didn't want to make things worse by insisting on an answer—would he give me one anyway? Instead, I sat and watched his profile as he drove, the concentration in his face, and the way in which his thoughts seemed so locked away from me.

Had he always been like this? Had he always lied like this? Because he must have said something to make that woman believe we weren't married. Made up some story.

Once again, I had that strange tilting feeling.

He's been hurt, I reminded myself. Some soldiers never properly recovered. The guns and the horror were forever with them, and they learned to cope in different ways, or failed to cope at all. I pictured again the sight of him crouched beneath the window just this morning, shaking, as the farmer fired his shotgun.

This was the new Owen, and I had to accept he may never be completely the same again. I had to rebuild my relationship with him, taking into account these uncomfortable quirks.

He took the next corner fast, causing the car to slide a little on the wet road. I grasped the dashboard with a little shriek, and he laughed.

He turned to me and grinned. "Hold on," he warned me, and then we were flying. And I forgot everything in the thrill of the moment.

Florence was out when we arrived in Easton Street. She was probably at the hospital. Despite the way she liked to pretend she was a society girl with nothing in her head but parties and having a good time, I knew better. She wanted to help people, and she had made friends at the hospital who were very unlike her usual crowd. She was one of those people who found it easy to slip between worlds, and who paid scant attention to the social mores others in her fashionable crowd insisted were so important.

The journey from Belsham had tired me out. I considered lying down on the bed for a while. After Owen had carried our cases up to our room, he had gone to put the car away in the garage in the mews. My gaze rested on the cases and I hesitated, then sighed. Unpacking would only take a moment and then I could properly rest. I quickly put away my own belongings and then turned to Owen's.

When I opened his case up, I saw something tucked down on one side. I recognised it at once. It was one of the shepherdesses that stood on Dad's mantelpiece. I reached in and took it out, holding it in the palm of my hand. It was one of the smaller statues. This one had a skirt with a bustle and a crook in her hand, while her saucy lips were lifted in a painted smile.

Seeing the piece here, out of its familiar surroundings, threw me for a moment. Then something else caught my eye. A family of ducks poorly made in cheap porcelain. When I picked them up, I saw they were stamped with the name of the pub we had stopped at for lunch. I remembered them being for sale in the bar—I had noticed them when we went inside to order our meal. Owen had gone back to ask for more drinks at some point. Had he bought them? Or…

"Emilia?"

His voice made me jump, and I closed the case more out of reaction than intent. I had my back to the bedroom door so I didn't hear him come in to the room.

"What are you doing?"

"I was going to unpack," I said, moving away now, straightening the quilt on the bed. My heart was thumping.

"That's all right. I'll do it," he replied. "No hurry." He pushed his case to one side and then stretched his arms out, yawning. He tilted his head and smiled indulgently at me. "Come here," he said softly.

Did I ask him what he was doing with my mother's shepherdess and the ducks from the pub? Did I insist he tell me what was going on?

No, I didn't. I was just too grateful to know he wanted me. I walked into his arms and let him hold me against his warm chest, and when he kissed me, I kissed him back.

This is what is important, I told myself. Owen and Emilia. Our love was strong enough to get through these turbulent waters and find sanctuary again.

Later, after we'd made love, I heard Florence come back. The front door closed and I heard her call up the stairs. I lifted my head drowsily.

"Stay here and sleep," Owen murmured, kissing me, and then he was gone. I lay in our bed, my body relaxed and pleasantly aching. I glanced at the window and saw that it was raining outside now, the sound soft and peaceful. I felt...content. Hopeful. Everything, I told myself, was going to be all right.

Their voices drifted up to me, and I heard Florence laugh. She sounded a long way away. But then, just as I was drifting off, I saw Dr

McIvor's dark eyes peering into mine. And his voice, fading, fading…

There will be a price to pay.

TWELVE

"I'M GOING TO throw a party," Florence announced the next morning, her grey eyes bright. "In my brother's honour."

I glanced sideways at Owen, thinking that maybe he didn't want a party in his honour. "I thought we had one last week." The Owen I knew was always averse to fuss.

"But that wasn't a *proper* one. I want all of our friends here. I want all of us to celebrate Owen being alive and home again."

To my surprise, Owen turned his head and grinned. "Sounds like fun."

Straight away, she began to list the guests she was going to invite, while Owen nodded. There was a moment when she had to admit that several of them hadn't come back from the war, and their heady excitement began to dip and waver, but soon they were laughing again and making their plans.

A knock at the door came, but neither of them moved, either ignoring it or too busy to hear it, so I went to open it.

As I reached for the latch, I suddenly had a vison of Dr McIvor's dark eyes and my hand shook. But that was silly. He wouldn't come here. He had taken advantage of me and pretended to be capable of something that was utterly impossible. Owen was back, but it was not through the supernatural machinations of the spiritualist church. I opened the door.

The owner of the *Courier*, Sir Richard Laurens, smiled at me, his jowly cheeks mottled from the cold. "Emilia!" There were rain droplets on the shoulders of his cashmere coat. "I say, such wonderful news! I couldn't believe it when I heard. Is he here?"

I let him in and closed the door behind him. He was already trotting down to the kitchen and I heard his excited greeting. By the time I reached them, he had the much larger Owen's hand in a hard clasp, while Florence looked on with tears in her eyes.

A fresh pot of coffee was made and I cooked eggs and bacon for anyone who wanted it, which turned out to be everyone. While I worked, I listened to their conversation. Sir Richard wanted Owen to give an interview, an exclusive for the *Courier*.

"It's a miracle and people need to hear about it. In these times with so many dead… so much grief… your story will give our readers hope."

Owen shook his head, and kept shaking it. In the end, he got up and walked out of the room. I heard the door slam. When he first came home he had loved being the focus of everyone, but now he was being more like the Owen I had married.

Sir Richard stared after him and I could see he found it frustrating that Owen was so resistant.

"You know how Owen is. He never liked being the centre of attention."

"I know. He always went on about how it wasn't about him when he was writing his stories from the front lines, but I need that story, Emilia," Sir Richard said with a determined set to his mouth. "And he does too. It will help get him back into the business. The war is over. We want him writing about life in London now. The new world. Good stories, optimistic, but honest. It's his honesty that has always shone through, it is what makes him such a good journalist."

I bit my lip. I didn't want to say it aloud, but Owen didn't seem quite so honest anymore. I remembered the shepherdess in his suitcase. It seemed innocuous enough, but it was so unlike my scrupulously honest Owen.

"I'll talk to him," I said.

"He needs to come back in to work," Sir Richard told me as I showed him to the door. "I can't hold his job forever."

"Hasn't he… I thought he'd been in?" Owen had told me that he had. I was sure of it.

"Not so far. He called me on the telephone to explain he was back, but not a word apart from that. Doesn't he realise how big his story is? Everyone wants to talk to him."

"He just needs time. Being home again after all he's been through must feel quite surreal. I-I'll remind him he has a job to do, Sir Richard." I heard my voice wobble.

He pretended not to notice. "It will help him to talk about it," he said stubbornly. "Get it out of his system."

I understood why he was so insistent. He had a newspaper to publish, and Owen's story was huge, but Owen was also part of the team. That he was still wanted there, that his job was still open, was a miracle in itself.

"I'll talk to him," I said again and watched Sir Richard walk away before closing the door. The house grew quiet apart from Florence busily telephoning people about the upcoming party.

"Saturday," I overheard her say. "Bring plenty of booze!" She laughed at whatever was said in reply. I knew I should talk to her about this new development with Owen, but at the same time it seemed unfair to weigh her down with what I had come to think of as my burden. I should be able to handle it myself, sort it out myself, make Owen better by myself.

I climbed the stairs to the bedroom, but Owen wasn't there. I thought I knew where he had gone. He'd taken the Daimler out as he always did these days when he was trying to clear his head. Would he listen to me when he returned? I had promised Sir Richard I would talk to him, but that didn't mean he would agree to listen to either of us.

There was a small, hard kernel inside me whenever I thought about confronting Owen. I rubbed my stomach where the ache was worst. Dread. Something I had never felt before when it came to my husband. And now I felt it all too often.

Florence had insisted I needed a new dress. Something celebratory and special. Something spectacular. She smiled when she said it, but I had the niggling feeling that what she really meant, was she wanted to remind the guests why Owen had married a country mouse like me. I wanted to ask her if he'd said something to her, but at the same time I wasn't sure I wanted to hear her answer.

I went shopping anyway, telling myself it would be good to get away from her frantic preparations and Owen's brooding silence.

I had managed to speak to him as Sir Richard asked, but although he'd listened and agreed to think about it, he hadn't been in to work yet and had refused to take any phone calls. It was as if he didn't want anything to do with the *Courier* or the job he once loved. Perhaps it reminded him too much of the war, and yet surely the fact that his boss wanted him back… wasn't that a good thing? Perhaps he worried he could no longer write the pieces that had made him so popular?

Sometimes I didn't understand him at all.

I spent a lot of time worrying about Owen while he was out in his car. He'd driven all the way to the south coast a few days ago where, he told me, he'd stood on the cliffs and looked over the channel and thought of his days during the war. I'd expected him to be upset by that, but instead he was grinning as if he'd won a prize.

"That'll show them," he'd said, and then he

was kissing me, and I let him distract me. He was like his old self again, and all my worries melted away. Owen still wanted me, and it was a relief. At moments like these I knew everything would be all right. Because if he started to push me away, I wasn't sure what I would do.

London's streets were wet from a rain shower, but the sun was trying to show through. I glimpsed the dress in the window of Dickins and Jones, and my steps slowed until I stood, staring through the glass. Rose coloured satin with lace at the hem, sleeveless and with a low back. It was daring, but I knew it would suit my curves and my colouring. It was also probably rather expensive, but I didn't care. I wanted Owen to look at me in that possessive manner that was becoming more and more necessary to my peace of mind.

The very thought of how he made love to me, rough and desperate, caused awareness to tingle in my spine. He could still be tender but increasingly he was forceful. As if he were dying to have me again, to make up for all the months we had spent apart. I found this new passion attractive, because I was desperate too. And because I liked it. Which conflicted me, made me feel as if, in some way, I was being unfaithful to the considerate gentleman Owen used to be.

I had discovered a book in the library about soldiers serving in the Crimean war, and the effect their experiences had had on them. There was a lot about Florence Nightingale, which made me smile, because my Florence was nothing like that dour, iconic woman. I hadn't really been looking for information on war damaged soldiers, but had been returning a novel that was due, when I saw this book on the shelves, and thought it might be helpful.

But as I read it, I realised that so many of the Crimean symptoms seemed to fit with Owen. Often the men who had survived had changed, often beyond all recognition. It was as if some fundamental alteration had taken place. Acknowledging it to myself was a relief but also depressing, because I was beginning to suspect that the Owen I had kissed and sent away was gone forever.

I had been lost in a daydream, staring blindly through the shop window, but now something caught my eye. I blinked and suddenly I was wide awake. A figure stood behind me. It was unfocussed, cloudy, and for a moment I thought it must be a smudge on the glass itself. With a frown, I took a step closer to the window and looked again. And I saw that the blurry smear was actually a man.

Owen.

He was standing behind me, at my shoulder, but the haziness made it seem as if he was in a cloud of steam. I froze in shock and confusion. A few masked shoppers walked past behind me but took no notice of me or the apparition behind me. Confused and shaken, I stared into his eyes. He was slightly clearer now, but still blurred at the edges, as if his body was bleeding into the surroundings. As if he were a watercolour painting that had been rained on.

I wanted to turn my head and see if he was really there. But I couldn't move. I feared if I had turned, he would have vanished instantly.

I was locked in this moment where time meant nothing, trying to understand it.

The expression on his face was... *frantic*. Distraught. This was the embodiment of the man I had heard speak through Anna Ward. This was the Owen I had listened to at the seance and who then promised anything and everything to have returned to me.

His mouth moved as if trying to speak, his eyes wide and desperate. I felt tears on my cheeks above my mask, because this was so horrible. Owen wanted my help. He wanted to tell me something. Why couldn't I hear him?

A tram rumbled behind me, and I was jolted out of whatever trance state I had been in. The moment was broken. When I looked at the reflection in the window again, there was only a London street at my back. Owen was gone.

I didn't buy the dress. I went into a Lyons tearoom and sat down and tried to still my trembling nerves. Had I been dreaming? Was I in a trance? The word brought back memories of Anna Ward and the seance, and Owen's voice forced from her straining throat.

He wants to speak to you. For a moment, I was back on the bus that first day in London, looking into Miss Ward's compassionate eyes.

I wanted to talk to her again. Who else would understand what had just happened, or be able to offer me some sort of explanation? I wanted to ask her questions, but at the same time I knew I couldn't go back to Tottenham Court Road.

There will be a price to pay.

The truth was, I was afraid to.

THIRTEEN

FLORENCE'S PARTY WAS a wild affair. So many people were crammed into our house there was barely room to move. Alcohol flowed freely and music filled the building. Eddie was there, looking as if he'd rather be somewhere else, but at the same time determined to stay in case Florence needed his support.

I wasn't sure she did; she seemed so in her element.

I had met Eddie a couple of times by now and I liked him. He appeared to be genuinely in love with my sister-in-law—I'd seen him wrap his coat around her when she shivered, or hold her hand when she became overwhelmed. He didn't talk about his job, even when some of her friends pestered him in snarky voices about some of his more colourful cases. *Amuse us!* And when he refused, they ignored him. He was vastly different from Florence's previous boyfriends and that seemed a good thing.

That night at the party, surrounded by laughing, chattering people we barely knew, I felt more out of place than ever.

"Are you all right?" he asked me.

I grimaced. "Is it that obvious? Sorry, blame the champagne."

There seemed to be buckets of it, a never-ending flow. I didn't normally think about how different Owen and Florence were to me, their lives, their upbringing, their wealth. It was at times like this that I remembered.

Eddie drew on his cigarette, the smoke drifting into my face when he blew it out, and I wished I could go outside and take in some fresh air. "Florence's friends think she's slumming," he said wryly. "That I'm not good enough for her."

I looked at him. Eddie was obviously well educated and middle class, perhaps more than middle class. I wondered if he was like Owen and Florence, privileged but socially aware, wanting to put something back.

"I disagree," I said thoughtfully. "You two are very much alike. At least in the ways that matter."

Loud laughter came from the stairs in the hallway, and I looked up. Owen had a group around him, and he was lifting his glass to the ceiling. "Have I thanked God yet?" he asked.

"You've thanked everyone else," a woman with bright red lipstick giggled.

"Thank you, God!" he roared, bubbly sloshing from his glass, and everyone fell about laughing.

I turned back to Eddie and found him looking at me as if waiting for a cue. I didn't have one, so I pretended to nonchalantly sip my champagne. Owen drunk and in the midst of a party was something I had never seen before, and it made me as uneasy as the Owen who lied and drove too fast and stole things.

After a search in the bedroom, I'd found where he put the shepherdess and the ducks. They were in an old wooden box in his closet, hidden at the bottom among his shoes. That I was searching in his things, spying on him, made me feel slightly ill. But I told myself I had to do it.

Owen was not himself, that much was clear. Understanding what he was going through, why I had had the vision outside the dress store… I wanted to make sense of it all. I needed to know what was happening to my husband.

As well as the items I knew about there were half a dozen others. Little things, inexpensive things, that he must have picked up somewhere. Among them was a cheap tarnished locket, a wooden steamship with *Souvenir of Southampton* stamped on it, and some equally random trinkets. I put them all back just as I found them.

It made no sense. Technically, he had stolen them—I was sure of that—yet they were worthless. Even my mother's porcelain shepherdess was only of sentimental value. Stealing these things seemed so senseless. I knew from my research on war trauma that kleptomania was a symptom. Was that what this was?

The party went on well into early morning. Eventually, people began to leave, some very drunk and helped by others who were relatively sober. Eddie stuck to Florence's side as if standing guard, which seemed to amuse her. She kept turning around and looking up at him from her spot on the sofa, cigarette holder in one hand, drink in the other, and bursting into laughter. He smiled back but didn't move.

It had the desired effect.

Florence's admirers drifted away, looking disgruntled, and the last time I looked at her she was holding Eddie's hand and smiling up at him in an entirely different way.

I hadn't seen Owen for a while. I began a search of the house, so much easier now than a few hours ago when there had been barely room to move. A man seated on the stairs, leaning his head against the bannisters, said that he'd seen Owen outside on the front steps. "Him and his strange friend," he'd added.

"What friend?"

When he didn't have an answer, I turned away.

I found Owen outside. He was sitting in the cold darkness of early dawn, as he smoked and stared down the street. Was there someone walking away? The shadows made it impossible to be certain, but I thought it was a man. And something about his outline made me think of Dr McIvor which was plainly ridiculous.

For a moment I watched Owen, wondering how it was possible to feel so much love for him and yet be so apprehensive and confused at the same time. Owen and I had never had a turbulent relationship before, but that's how it now felt.

His dark hair was rumpled, his collar askew, and his shoulders bowed as he leaned forward with his elbows on his thighs. The cigarette smoke drifted around him. A shout came from inside, followed by drunken laughter. He lifted his head. That was when I saw the lipstick on his neck, just below his jaw. Bright red smeared greasily onto his skin.

A drunken kiss at a party, I told myself. It was nothing. I had been to enough of Florence's parties to know better than to attribute anything more to a drunken kiss than a momentary loss of control. And yet seeing that lipstick on his skin made me feel… nauseous. As if my worst fears had been handed ammunition to use against me at a later date.

"Owen?" I took a step forward, and he turned to look at me.

"Emilia," he said, his voice a little slurred. "My dearest little wife. Where have you been?"

It was ridiculous to point out I had been at the party too, so I didn't. "Are you ready for bed?" I asked him.

His eyes slid over me in that way that was both exciting and unnerving. That now familiar tingle raced up my spine. Was it desire? Perhaps. Fear? A mixture of both?

"I think I might be," he answered. Then his eyes crinkled at the corners as he smiled. "Sorry I'm a bit the worse for wear, but it's not every day you get to celebrate your return from the dead."

"I'm glad. Florence didn't miss anyone, did she? She tried to invite everyone you knew."

He gave a bark of laughter. "I hardly recognised most of them and forgot the names of those I did, but they didn't seem to care."

"It was a marvellous party. You must thank her."

He stood up, using the railing on the stairs to

support himself, and tossed the spent cigarette aside. "I'd forgotten what it was like to have a sister." He said it as if talking to himself. The next moment he was looking at me, his face pinched, eyes sharp. I kept smiling and he gave a self deprecating laugh. "I'm sorry. I'm drunk," he said, but I wondered if he was really as drunk as he seemed.

What did it matter? I put my arm around him and helped him inside. The music was still playing from the sitting room, "Till We Meet Again", and Florence was there with Eddie, swaying together. I suspected he was holding her up at this point, but it still looked very romantic, the way they were meshed against each other, her head resting on his shoulder, his lips pressed to her hair.

Something like envy twisted in my heart. I wanted it to be me and Owen dancing like that.

FOURTEEN

FLORENCE WAS CRYING. I stood in the front doorway, my shopping in one hand, the house key still in the other. I set down the bread and hurried through the house, following the sobs into the kitchen. Florence was sitting at the table with her head in her hands, and I flew across to put my arms around her. Florence's shoulders shook and she rested her head, still covered by her hands, against my shoulder.

"What is it?" I cried. "Flo? What's wrong?"

"I'm a fool," she gasped. "I shouldn't have said anything. It's all my fault."

"What did you say?"

"I… Owen. I said it to Owen, and he was so angry. So angry. He said things…"

I felt myself go cold. Owen had made his sister *cry*? "What did you say?"

She hiccupped. "The car. Father's car, the Daimler. There was a big dent in the front and one of the headlamps is squashed. Owen must have run into something. He drives too fast, Emilia! Too recklessly. Really, I'm more worried about him than the car, but I said he needed to slow down and take more care. I said that Father…Father would never have driven so wildly."

It was true, I had thought it so myself, although I hadn't realised he'd had an accident. "But he wasn't hurt?"

Florence lifted her head, her eyes swollen, her nose red. "He wasn't hurt. He told me it was his car and he could do whatever he liked with it and if he wanted to drive at eighty-five miles per hour through London, he would."

That was a ridiculous speed. And dangerous enough even without being on a busy London thoroughfare. "What happened exactly?"

Florence shrugged. She was still in her robe, not yet properly dressed for the day. I had been up early and bought some bread from the French baker down the road as a treat. When I'd left Owen had still been in bed and Florence had been pottering around the kitchen, boiling the kettle and making tea.

"He said he took a corner too fast, but no one was hurt. Then when I asked him to be more careful, to slow down… I reminded him that he never would have behaved in such a foolish manner before he came back. And he said it sounded as if I wished he hadn't. Come back, I mean. And I said that perhaps I did." Her shoulders shook on a sob. She pressed her fingertips to her mouth. "I was angry," she whispered. "I didn't mean it… of course I didn't mean it. But he's been so strange, Emilia. So different."

"What happened then?"

"He shouted at me and called me a 'snooty bitch', and then he stormed out."

It was worrying, but I tried to tell myself that Owen had been hurt. Florence's insensitive words had set him off. "Do you know where he is now?"

"He went out. I don't think he took the car, I doubt it's driveable at the moment. He'll have to get it fixed."

Florence glanced at the kitchen clock and stood up, pulling her robe close around her. "I need to get dressed. Eddie is coming to pick me up."

"On a workday?"

"He works at odd hours," she explained. Before she could get to the door, I stopped her.

"I think Owen needs to see a doctor." It was a relief to say the words at last. I'd been thinking this for some time, but was afraid of what Florence would say if I suggested it.

Florence turned to look at me, her face still a mess, and shook her head. "We can't do that, Emilia. He'll think we… He's been through enough, we just need to be patient. I know he'll be himself again soon."

I stared back at her. "But you think he's not himself now?" I asked carefully. "That he's changed?"

Florence looked guilty. "I suppose he has, but so many men who've come back from the war have changed. I see it all the time at the hospital, Emilia. There are some awfully sad cases."

"I'm not saying he has shell shock, but there's something wrong, Florence. Do you think you could get me an appointment to talk to someone? Just you and me, not Owen. I think it would help both of us to feel better if we heard someone else's opinion on what was happening with him. Discreetly, of course."

For a moment Florence looked as if she would say no, then she sighed, and the resistance drained out of her. "I can try. I know one who would see you, if I asked. But Emilia—"

"Florence, maybe he just needs some advice. I know he says he doesn't, but maybe he does. I want to explain to someone what is happening, and at least then we might have an idea of how to proceed, how to react when he does these uncharacteristic things. He upset you. Called you a foul name. That isn't like Owen."

Florence's face went still, but I could see she was struggling with her thoughts. She didn't want to upset her brother more than she already had. Perhaps she was right, but I couldn't let this situation go on any longer. Florence had always let Owen take the lead, he had taken care of her, and I could see that the idea of her doing the same for him, turning their relationship on its head, was difficult for her.

"Very well," she said at last. Then, with determination, "I'll do it."

"Good."

When she was gone, I sat down at the table and stared at the window. Rain dripped down the pane, making patterns on the walls against the light. I admit I was relieved. I could talk to someone and perhaps they would tell me that

Owen's behaviour was all perfectly normal in the circumstances. That it would go away with time.

But what about the ghost in the window? The seance and Dr McIvor and his promise to bring Owen back from the dead?

Nonsense. It was simply not possible for the dead to return. At best, the doctor would call me foolish, at worse, he would lock me in a padded cell.

Owen was here with me, alive. I needed to concentrate on that. Yes, Owen wouldn't approve if he found out, but it was all in an effort to help him. He would have to understand that.

Florence managed to get an appointment for the following afternoon. Owen used to say that Florence could get anything from anybody if she used her powers of persuasion—it was a joke they shared. Now I wondered if jokes like that were even possible between them anymore.

That Owen had changed so much toward his own sister was one of the reasons I needed to talk to a medical professional.

It was late in the afternoon when we went. I'd thought Owen might ask where we were going and had prepared a story about a shopping expedition, but he wasn't there and I wasn't sure where he had gone. The car was getting fixed at a mechanic's and he had taken Florence's car. I'd seen her hand over the keys without protest.

Florence looked wane and a little afraid, as if

she were concerned that Owen might find out what we were up to. The old Owen, the one who went away, would have understood she was trying to help him, but who knew how our Owen would react now?

We caught the bus, sitting together in silence as the late afternoon grew darker and heavy rain came down. It did nothing to raise our spirits. I wished the summer would come.

I had checked the secret stash in the closet again this morning and it had grown. There was a broken lighter and a lipstick in there now, bright red, not unlike that worn by the woman at the party. I stood looking down at it and felt something wobble inside me.

Where had these things come from? Where had Owen been when he slipped them so casually into his pocket? I might have been able to pretend at first that it was a mistake, a moment of forgetfulness, but now... I no longer could. Was it something he did for his own amusement? But why? It made no sense to me.

"Have you ever known Owen to steal?" I blurted out the words to Florence before I could stop myself. I wanted her to tell me I was being silly, overreacting. That it was something Owen had done before and it was just some silly joke.

She didn't. She gasped. "Steal? Owen? No! Owen would never do that." Then, eying me strangely, "Why do you ask?"

I could lie, but I no longer wanted to. We were in this together now, for Owen's sake. "I found some things he must have taken."

"What things? That sounds rather odd," Florence said, "and not at all like Owen."

I nodded, suddenly deflated, and Florence took my hand in her gloved one. "This is why you wanted to see a doctor, isn't it?"

I sighed. "It's part of the reason."

When I looked at her again, she was staring ahead, her brow scrunched up with concern. We didn't speak as the bus chugged on toward St Thomas's.

Once there, Florence took me straight past the front desk, down a long corridor with squeaky linoleum and closed doors. She seemed to know her way around without hesitation and stopped at a door with a name on it, Dr Rayner, and knocked sharply. There was a muffled, "Come in."

Dr Rayner was a middle-aged man with steel grey hair and a three-piece suit. He looked tired, but his smile was warm, particularly when he saw Florence. She introduced me and we were seated. I wasn't sure where to begin, but the doctor seemed to know our story. I supposed Florence had told him, just as she had probably told everyone when Owen came home.

"His behaviour has changed," I blurted out. "I wanted to know if that is normal … I mean, is it…?" I left the sentence hanging.

He smiled kindly. "Is it normal for a man who has been through a terrible time, seen dreadful things and wondered every moment whether he would live through it to change dramatically? Yes, Mrs Flett, I think that is normal. I had a man in here the other day who couldn't stop shaking. The hospitals are full of them."

Owen was shaking that morning when the farmer was shooting at the crows. He'd been terrified. I could understand that, but the rest... Were they really all to do with his experiences in the war?

"I know about the some of the effects Owen might suffer," I said, before he could reassure me any further. "This is different."

"Why don't you tell me then, Mrs Flett?"

I glanced at Florence. I had kept aspects of Owen's strange behaviour from her, but now I just needed to tell someone. "He steals. Just little things, nothing worth much, but he has a cache of them. And he lies, I know he does. He doesn't remember a lot of the past, names and faces... He's different, and yet he's the same. He's reckless too. Careless. Owen was neither of those things."

"He wrecked his motor car," Florence added. "It's as if he doesn't care about dying anymore. That he defeated death once and now he thinks he's invincible."

"He's been horrible to Florence, and sometimes he says things to me that are completely out of character. Hurtful things. I try to tell myself he doesn't mean them, not really, but I'm beginning to think he does."

Dr Raynor was frowning. "Cases of brain trauma caused by physical injury due to shell attack are well documented. Now we are discovering that even men not caught in the heat of the action can be affected. So I suppose it's possible Mr Flett's personality has undergone changes. Perhaps even fundamental changes."

I remembered Dr McIvor talking about the connection between the flesh and the soul, but I suspected Dr Raynor would not want to hear any of that.

"Will he ever be Owen again?" Florence asked softly.

"I wish I could say he will, but this is a situation us doctors are still coming to terms with. You know, there are places he could go. We don't understand the condition all that well, but we are learning. He may be able to help us move forward in our understanding. The hospital in Queen Square…"

Florence looked horrified. She shook her head and thanked him. Afterwards, we walked slowly back down the corridor. "It wasn't exactly what you wanted to hear, was it?" Florence said.

"No."

"I feel ungrateful wishing that he was the same, when we're so lucky to have him home with us again."

I squeezed her hand. "I feel exactly the same."

"Should we tell him what we did?" Florence asked tentatively.

I shook my head. "I think we should keep it to ourselves." I said what Florence wanted to hear. She looked relieved and gave me a small smile.

"I think so too."

I hadn't told Dr Rayner everything. Recently, I had noticed something else about Owen. The thing I had been fearing.

The last few nights, Owen's urgent desire for me seemed to have cooled. He no longer pounced on me as soon as we went to bed, and last night when I reached out for him, he smiled and patted my hand and turned over. There had been a sympathetic, slightly puzzled look in his eyes, as if he felt sorry for me but couldn't be bothered. It hurt, it truly did.

I tried to tell myself that the doctor was right and I had to accept that the Owen who had come home may never be the man who had left it. He had experienced such horrific things. It was silly to be hurt because he wasn't as loving as he once was, and yet I couldn't help it. Maybe if he'd been distant from the very start, I wouldn't be so concerned, but that hadn't been the case.

When he'd come back, he had loved me, had wanted me. And now he didn't.

I remembered the smeared lipstick on his skin and the stolen lipstick in his closet. Was there someone else? It felt like a betrayal even thinking it. Owen had sworn to be true to me, to love, honour and obey me, and I had never had reason to doubt him.

Now I did.

Could I accept this new state of affairs? It wasn't unusual for men of Owen's class to have a mistress, although I would never have imagined Owen would hurt me like that. But if he did… would I be able to play the part required of me?

I wanted to say 'yes' but I wasn't sure I could. Because if he had come back to me against all odds, only for me to lose him to another woman, I might wish he had never come home at all.

FIFTEEN

EVENTUALLY, OWEN GAVE the interview to Sir Richard for the *Courier*. After being so reluctant at first, he suddenly had a complete turnaround and met the prospect with enthusiasm. I suspected part of that was because Sir Richard had agreed Owen would not write the piece himself. The interview took place at our house and Florence and I both listened as Owen answered questions about his time as a war correspondent, and his need to be more than a mouthpiece for the authorities.

"So, your reason for going to the front line, risking your life, was purely to write the truth?" the journalist asked.

Owen thought for a moment and then grinned. "Well, there was that," he said. "It was also a bloody lot more exciting than sitting around drinking tea with the old farts from *The Times* and the *Daily Express*."

The journalist seemed delighted by that, chuckling as he wrote down Owen's response. Owen glanced over at us and winked. Afterwards, there were some photos of him relaxing in the sitting room, and then the three of us together. Smiling. Happy.

"It'll be on the front page," Owen said confidently once the journalist left. "You wait and see."

He was right. It was on the front page two days later, a photo of Owen smiling at the camera, so handsome and relaxed, and the amazing story of his return from the dead. In fact, that was the headline, "Return from the Dead," which was a little over the top for the *Courier*, but Sir Richard had decided under the circumstances it was warranted.

Owen was as excited as a child at Christmas. His face and name were splashed all over the city. Florence seemed to find his behaviour adorable and amusing, but I could only see how much my husband had changed. The Owen I had married would have loathed the publicity, would have buried himself in his work or taken himself off to Belsham and hidden out with my father, talking about book plots by the fire, over brandy. This man basking in the limelight, soaking up the attention, was even more of a stranger than I'd thought.

Owen's car was fixed, and he'd been going out driving on his own again. If I asked, he'd tell me where he was going and I had no choice but to believe him, but I always wondered. His smile, his eye contact, his kiss on my cheek—they were all meant to inspire my trust in him. It was as if he had studied the ways to convince me of his honesty.

Yet I kept thinking about the lipstick and the ever-growing stash of stolen trinkets in the box in his closet. There were now several match books, the sort you found in nightclubs—Daltons and the Embassy, to name just two. I began to grow more and more desperate.

If I learned the truth about him, if I could prove he was lying, would that make me feel better? Of course it wouldn't. Yet it seemed better than burying my head in the sand and pretending everything was all right.

A couple of nights he didn't come home at all, showing up early in the morning to bathe and change. He'd say he was drinking with the journalists from the *Courier*, or he'd met up with some old friends … There was always a reason, nothing to worry about, and Owen certainly wasn't worried. He'd walk through the house, whistling, without a care in the world.

Time passed and then one evening the phone gave a shrill ring. It was right on supper time, and I hurried to answer it, leaving the others to finish their meal. Florence had been talking about Eddie and how busy he was with his job. Evidently, the crime rate had soared since the war ended, and I had noticed he was around less often as a result.

Owen had listened to her complaints with a smile on his face that wasn't quite nice. He'd responded to her, not with sympathy and good sense, but with little digs about the police in general and Florence's taste in men in particular. If she had noticed, then she hadn't taken the bait, or perhaps she was trying to ignore him, which only made his taunts worse.

"No man likes a woman who complains all the time," was the last thing I heard him say before I jumped up to answer the phone.

I would have suggested Florence answer the call, just to get her out of the room, but I thought it might be my father. I hadn't seen him for ages or heard from him either. I had meant to call him, but what would I say? My suggestions about visiting had been shrugged off by Owen. The last time I'd mentioned it, he'd frowned and said, "You go, Emilia. I thought we'd already decided that? I can't leave London."

He was probably right. He was easing himself back into his job at the *Courier*, although he was yet to write any articles for the newspaper. To explain his reluctance he said he hadn't found the right story yet. I could visit my father on my own, and even stay a while to help him, but something stopped me from taking that step. I suppose I was afraid that if I left Owen, he might consider himself free of me. He'd forget I existed. While I was still here with him, there was a chance I could turn things around, that just maybe I could make everything better.

"Mrs Flett?" The woman's voice on the other

end of the line was scratchy and not immediately recognisable.

"Yes?"

"This is Anna Ward."

I was silent. Anna Ward, the medium for the World Beyond spiritualist church. Hearing from her caused several emotions to rise inside me, and I wasn't sure how to respond.

"How did you get this number?"

"From the story in the newspaper. About Owen, your husband."

Once again, I struggled to find a reply. "What do you want?" I'm sure I sounded rude, but it was the best I could do.

"I need to talk to you, Mrs Flett. It's important." She sounded breathless, as if she had been running, or perhaps it was nerves. There was an urgency to her words that ramped up my anxiety. I didn't want to see her, then I realised quite suddenly that I really needed to talk to her about the image I had seen reflected in the shop window. I wanted her to explain how Owen could be a ghost when he was also a living, breathing man. Maybe hearing her fumble to make sense of it for me would remind me how ridiculous the whole idea had been, and then I could move on and have nothing more to do with her.

"Talk to me about what?" I asked. I could hear Florence's voice from the dining room, raised, angry. I needed to get back there and soothe her, divert Owen's sour mood. I needed…

"Mrs Flett, please. We need to meet somewhere. Alone." There were voices in her background too, and Anna lowered her voice to almost a whisper. I wondered where she was, who she was with, and why she didn't want them to hear her. "Don't bring your husband… or anyone else."

Something in her tone told me there was more to both our situations than I had suspected.

"All right," I said quietly. "I'll come."

We arranged to meet in two days' time, at a tea shop I knew in Oxford Street. As I hung up, I told myself that I just wanted to get it over with. Meet her, hear what she had to say, tell her I was no longer interested, and walk out. There was no point in telling anyone else, she was right in that. Not Florence, and certainly not Owen.

Owen looked up at me when I re-entered the room, as if he had read my mind, or saw the guilt on my face. I had never been particularly good at prevaricating, but of late I had got much better.

"Who was it?"

"My father," I said, knowing that would prevent him from asking any more questions.

Florence was still bubbling on about Eddie until Owen suddenly stood up, stopping her.

"Let me tell you what you need to do so that he takes more notice of you." He then leaned down and whispered something in her ear.

I saw Florence's face get hot and flushed, and her eyes widen with shock. She kept staring at him as he stepped back.

Owen chuckled. "Do *that*, and I promise you he will keep coming back for more." He then strolled out the door and closed it behind him. We could hear his footsteps hurrying up the stairs.

"Florence?" I asked. "What did he say?"

She still sat frozen in place, then shook her head a little wildly. "Nothing, it's nothing."

I asked again, but she wouldn't tell me what Owen had said. She just kept shaking her head as if trying to shake out the words he had whispered in her ear. It had to be something horrible, vulgar and inappropriate advice that a fond brother should not give to his little sister.

Anger spiralled up inside me, and I chased after Owen up the stairs, ignoring Florence when she called out to me.

Owen was in our bedroom. He had changed into grey flannel trousers and a tweed jacket. His hair was damp, as if he'd washed his face and run his fingers through the thick dark strands.

"Are you going out?" I asked, surprised, stopping myself from adding *again*.

He turned and gave me a beaming smile, his grey eyes glinting with excitement. "I'm meeting Sir Richard for a drink at the Black Duck." It was as if the conversation with Florence had never been. "There's talk about a book, Emmy."

It had been so long since he'd used his pet name for me.

I smiled back. This was good. A book would be good for Owen. Then I remembered his childlike excitement over the newspaper article and wondered if a book would only make him worse. He seemed to thrive on attention these days.

"That's wonderful," I said, putting feeling into the words. "Do you want me to come?"

He seemed to consider it, but we both knew he was just playing for time, because he never wanted me to come. "Perhaps not at this stage," he said, tapping his fingers on the base of the bed, impatient to be away. "We're just talking. Someone from John Lane, the publisher, is going to be there, so we'll have some drinks and a chat. No decisions or contracts at this stage. You know, they'll want your side of the story too."

He looked at me as if he thought I should be over the moon about that. "Oh."

"I'll get them to write it for you, if you like."

"Aren't you writing the book, Owen?"

He looked uncomfortable. "I think it's best if I get a ghost writer. The words just don't come the way they used to. He'll do a better job than me."

I stared at him in disbelief, not knowing what to say. He avoided my gaze as he picked up his wallet from the dressing table, glancing about to see if he'd forgotten anything.

"Owen," I said quietly, "what did you say to Florence just now? You upset her."

His expression tightened. "Then she shouldn't have asked for my advice."

"Of course she'd ask for your advice. She always has."

"Then maybe it's time she stopped." He bent to kiss me. I turned my face so that his lips only grazed my cheek. I heard him make an impatient groan, and then he walked away. I listened to his footsteps on the stairs, the familiar creak of the fourth tread. Voices in the hall, his and Florence's. She sounded angry or upset, perhaps both.

He said he was going out, but I didn't believe he was telling me the truth about where he was going. I didn't trust him, and I was sick and tired of burying my head in the sand. I wanted to know. Even if it destroyed me, shattered heart into tiny pieces, I wanted to know.

It was a spur of the moment thing, I told myself later. I hadn't planned it, not really. And yet perhaps, in my secret heart, I had been planning it all along.

I pulled on my coat and scarf and tucked my gloves into my pocket. As I turned, I caught a glimpse of myself in the mirror and realised the bright red scarf stood out far too much. I pulled it off and found a dark blue one before I went to the landing and waited in the shadows, listening to them argue.

"I don't understand you," Florence said. I could hear the tears in her voice. "I don't *know* you. Not anymore." Then I heard Owen's softer response, a chuckle as if he were laughing at her. The front door opened and closed.

Florence heard me come down the stairs and turned to look up, her face a mixture of fury and misery.

"Can I have the keys to your car?" I asked quickly.

She wiped a finger under her eyes where the tears were leaking out, making her eyeliner run. "Why?"

"I'm going somewhere."

"With Owen? Can't *he* drive?"

"No, not with him."

She stared back at me and I saw the truth slowly dawn on her face. "You're following him," she said. Before I could answer, she went to hall closet and took out her coat.

I nodded to her in solidarity. "He's going to the Black Duck, and I'm going to find some answers there." I heard the tone of my voice, the anguish and yearning. "He lies to me, Flo. All the time. And there's more, but I ... I just need to see for myself."

"You know, there was a time when I would have laughed at you, but now?" She looked miserable, her mouth turned down. Then she straightened her shoulders. "Come on then," she said. "Let's find out what my dear brother is up to."

SIXTEEN

WE DIDN'T SPEAK. Florence wouldn't tell me what Owen had said, and I didn't want to press the matter. She was such a free spirit, so it must have been something truly awful to shake her like this. But I was glad she was here with me. I realised now how very lost and alone I had felt over the past few months.

When we pulled up at the Black Duck, I could see Owen's red Daimler in the carpark area. Relief almost overwhelmed me. Maybe this was all a wild goose chase. Perhaps I had been fuelling my doubts with my vivid imagination, creating an insane story out of nothing.

Florence parked the car further down the street. The area around the pub was quite busy, with offices and shops taking up the street front, but the further we got from the pub, the poorer the surroundings became. This was a far cry from Easton Street.

"Well," Florence said into the silence that had fallen between us. "Shall we go and have a sticky beak?"

We couldn't see the pub from here, so we got out and strolled cautiously toward it, pretending for a moment to look in the window of a pawnbroker. The pub was next door, the glass steamed from the heat inside. There was a low hum of voices, glasses clinking, and someone singing off-key, but whenever one of the patrons opened the door to go in, or come out, the noise rose tenfold.

Despite it being the middle of the week, the establishment was busy. Journalists from the *Courier* and some of the other newspapers often congregated here after work. Owen had brought me with him a few times before, shortly after we had been married. He said I gave him an excuse to get away before things got too boring, but it was said in an affectionate way. What he actually was saying was he would rather be with me. This new Owen hadn't said that in a while.

I dug my gloved hands deeper into my pockets.

"What do we do now?" asked Florence. I could barely see her. She stood at the corner of a narrow laneway between the pub and the pawnbroker, where the shadows were deepest. I had seen the bins and other detritus from the pub down there. The smell made me think they weren't emptied very often.

"Honestly, I didn't think he'd be here. I thought…" I chewed my lip. "Maybe we should just go home."

"No. Not yet." I saw her reach into her purse and take out her cigarette case. She opened it and lit one before breathing out, the scent of tobacco drifting around us. It was at least more pleasant than the rubbish in the lane.

"I could go inside," I said after a moment. "Pretend I've come to join him."

She paused with the cigarette halfway to her lips. "Did he ask you to?"

"No," I admitted. "He said not to."

"Then don't," she said.

I don't know how long we stood outside, our feet turning into blocks of ice. In my rush to leave, I hadn't thought to change into my outdoor shoes. Every now and again Florence also gave a shudder as she smoked cigarette after cigarette.

Opposite the pub were three women leaning against the wall of a churchyard. They were smoking and chatting together. It took me a while to guess their profession because they looked rather like bored housewives. Bored and desperate, I now suspected, because who would want to sell their body if it wasn't an absolute necessity?

I was about to tell Florence we really should go, that this was becoming ridiculous, when the door to the pub opened yet again. This time, Owen and Sir Richard stepped out. They stood on the street, talking, and every now and again glanced back at the door as if they were waiting for someone. Soon they were joined by a third person, a woman.

I didn't recognise her, but I had not been to the *Courier* offices for nearly two years. Perhaps it was Sir Richard's wife? Although I thought she was too young for that. Blonde and slim, dressed for an evening out rather than an after work do in a pub. His secretary? Or perhaps it was someone from the publisher? Owen had said someone from John Lane would be there.

I heard Owen laugh as they stood in a little group. The woman leaned in and tapped his arm in a teasing reprimand. Eventually Sir Richard walked off, waving a goodbye, leaving Owen and the woman together.

"Are we going to follow him?" Florence whispered. I saw her eyes shining in the light from the window. "What if he goes home and we're not there?"

"I can always say I went out with you and Eddie," I said.

She didn't reply, but gave me a little sideways glance. Perhaps she was surprised at how easily I had learned to lie. She wasn't the only one.

Owen and his friend were smoking now, and he stamped his feet to keep warm. She leaned in close to say something and he laughed, easily, as if he was happy in her company.

"Maybe we should just go home," I said, trying not to sound as shaken as I felt. Owen lifted a hand and tucked a strand of blonde hair back behind her ear. It was an intimate gesture rather than a friendly one. My stomach ached. Was I reading too much into this? Or was this proof of what I had feared all along?

"No," Florence responded in a tight voice. "We can't pretend we haven't seen this. I understand, Emilia, truly I do. It would be nice to pretend, but we can't. We need to see what happens next. We need to be sure."

I nodded, unable to speak. I knew what was

going to happen. Owen and the woman would leave together and go to her house, and then…

A car pulled up outside the pub. The woman tapped Owen's shoulder and smiled. She hurried across the footpath with a wave and tossed away her cigarette before she climbed in. The car pulled away and she was gone.

Relief. I almost sagged with it.

"Just a friend then," Florence whispered beside me, and I heard her own relief.

The Owen who had left had been the one reliable thing in our lives, always honest and true. And yet here, now, we no longer believed that because the man who had returned was neither.

Owen stood and watched the car pull away, then took out his cigarette case and lit up. The smoke drifted toward us. I'd dismissed it at first as a habit picked up on the front line, but now it was just one more thing that made this new Owen different from the old one. There was a line between the two of them and it was growing more defined by the day.

He glanced in our direction. We were deep in the shadows now, safe I thought, but still my heart jumped. Had he seen us? Did he recognise us? I couldn't breathe. Florence grabbed my arm and dragged me into the laneway with her. The smell of the bins made me feel as though I might vomit.

We heard his footsteps on the flagstones, moving closer. As he walked by the alley I saw his shape, his silhouette, and then he was gone. A minute ticked by before we dared to peer around the corner. Florence shook so badly that I put my arm around her shoulders to hold her.

He was heading towards the prostitutes who were leaning against the churchyard wall. I saw them stop gossiping and straighten up, their faces turned to my husband like lionesses scenting prey.

"Emilia," Florence said. "Perhaps you are right. We should go."

I shook my head. I couldn't have looked away even had I wanted to—and I did want to. Owen stopped in front of the group, and I heard laughter as they shuffled together, tossing comments back and forth. He offered out his cigarettes and I saw them take one each, lighting up when Owen flicked his lighter. I could see his smiling face in the glow. The planes of his cheekbones and brow, the untidy fall of his dark hair, his eyes bright pinpoints of light.

This was a stranger in my husband's body.

"Perhaps he's going to write a story?" Florence suggested. "Gathering material for some story he's planning."

I didn't even bother to dignify that with an answer.

They stood there, talking, smoking, and it was the longest ten minutes of my life. Then Owen ground his cigarette butt beneath his heel and, with a final word, turned and walked away. Florence slumped beside me in relief.

"He's going to his car," I whispered. "We should follow him."

She didn't reply this time, just stumbled after me. By the time we reached her car, the Daimler was passing us, and by the time Florence pulled out to follow, Owen was at the end of the street.

I leaned forward, worried we would lose him. I couldn't let this go. There was a terrible urgency inside me. Was he going home now, home to me? Was his evening over, or had he just been marking time?

He turned onto another street, heading to the East End, where the dilapidated houses far outnumbered the others. Poverty leeched from the dirty lanes and courts. Street lamps here were few and far between. Florence cruised along, keeping a distance between us and him, her gaze fixed on the familiar red car. Owen made another turn, and again we followed, silent except for our breathing. It was very cold, and my hands felt frozen, but I no longer cared.

Five more minutes and he pulled to a stop outside a decrepit tenement. In fact, the whole street was very rundown. Dark houses loomed everywhere in the star filled night, with the occasional light shining in a grubby window. Centuries of poverty and dirt were everywhere, made only worse by the unemployment of the returning soldiers.

Florence had turned her headlamps off, making us invisible, and she came to a halt several houses back from Owen. We watched as he opened his car door and climbed out. He paused and glanced back over his shoulder, as if he had sensed us. We both froze, waiting.

"He can't see us," Florence assured me.

I looked at her, and wondered again why we were so frightened that he might.

When I turned back, Owen's car had stopped. There was a squeal, and a child came running out of the shadows and into his arms. Surely it was too late for children to still be awake? Florence and I stared in confusion as Owen held the child and lifted them up in the air.

Did Owen know a family in this rundown tenement? Was he visiting a friend? He had set the girl down—I thought it was a girl—and now they were walking up the stairs together. He opened the street door and went in.

Florence moved her car further along the curb so that we were directly opposite where Owen had vanished.

I looked up at the front of the building, not really expecting to see anything. He could be visiting any of the many rooms in the tenement. But there was a light in one of the windows, and I found my gaze fixed there. It was the sort of low, intimate light made by a gas lantern as opposed to the harsh glare of electricity.

A dark shape appeared at the window, and I knew from the shape that it was Owen. I saw him remove his coat and reach for the blind, just as a woman appeared at his side. As the blind slid down to cover the window, I saw them merge.

I knew now. I knew the very worst. There was nothing I could do to rationalise this as I had the many other things Owen had done. He was breaking my heart and Owen, my Owen, would never have done that.

Someone blew their car horn and I jumped. We were driving now and I hadn't even realised it. Florence was speeding out of the maze of narrow streets. I wondered if she even knew where she was going. Fortunately, the next turn brought us into more familiar territory.

"Do you still think there's some explanation?" My voice was cold and bitter, and it didn't even sound like me. "Another story he's gathering material for?"

"Emilia..."

"I can't pretend anymore," I said. "This isn't the man I married."

"We have to confront him." Florence sounded desperate. "We should go back and confront him, Emilia. Shouldn't we?"

"He'll only lie," I said wearily. "He'll have an excuse."

I had asked for Owen to come back to me, but this wasn't the man I'd longed for. Was this the price McIvor had spoken of?

Florence drove aimlessly, as if to put distance between the grim reality of what we had seen and the pleasant lie of our cosy house in Easton Street. It was very late when we finally pulled up in front of the door. She let me out, but she wasn't going to join me. She would be staying at Eddie's tonight.

"Will you be all right?" she asked, before I shut the door.

"I might go to Belsham for a while," I said wearily. "In a day or so." I'd remembered that I still had an appointment to meet Anna Ward, something that now felt more urgent than ever.

Florence didn't argue. "I'll be back in the morning," she said. "We can talk then."

I went to the door and turned the key. The house seemed very still but there was a light coming from the sitting room. I wasn't sure if we had left it on, but in our haste we probably had. As I reached the door, meaning to turn it off, I froze and caught my breath in shock.

Owen was seated on the sofa, drinking whiskey from a heavy glass. He must have heard me, but he finished his sip before he looked up. I could smell the mingled scents of tobacco and perfume on him. He turned to me before I could speak, although I had no idea what I was going to say.

He knew. Perhaps he had known from that moment outside the pub when he had glanced in Florence and my direction, or perhaps he had recognised her car on the street. Or maybe it was the expression on my face that gave me away.

"You really are a glutton for punishment," he said in an idle way, sloshing his brandy back and forth, watching the light transform it.

"I don't know what you mean," I said, my voice stilted and low.

"Don't you?" He eyed me a moment more and then grinned. And it was Owen's grin, but behind the smile and the familiar features, was a different man from the one I loved. I knew it, and I wondered how I had ever convinced myself otherwise. This was a stranger, an impostor, and imagining going to bed with him brought a curl of nausea to my stomach.

"I'll sleep in the spare room," I said.

He gave a soft laugh. "No need on my account, wife. I think we've exhausted your repertoire in bed."

I ignored him and went up the stairs, my legs stiff. Once I met with Anna Ward I would move back to my father's house, although there was still Florence to consider. Could I really leave Florence with him, here, alone? I decided I would persuade her to leave too. Have her go to Eddie. I trusted Eddie.

The spare room was full of items cleared from elsewhere, crowded and uncomfortable. The bed felt stiff and unused. It didn't matter. Anything was better than being with Owen. I lay down without undressing, wrapping my coat tight about me. I was cold, so cold. Cold on the outside, and colder on the inside.

I could have dozed, although it didn't feel like it. Sometime later, the door cracked open. I smelt that combination of tobacco smoke and perfume. I held my breath. "You know I didn't mean it," Owen said quietly. "Come to bed with me, Emilia."

I felt as if his voice were velvet, brushing against my skin, so warm and soothing. The impostor sounded like Owen, and for an instant, all the doubts crept back in. I'd made a mistake and everything was all right. Yes, somehow my vivid imagination had misconstrued everything. I could go to him now, and we would be all right again.

But I was lying to myself. I had been lying all along. Because I knew. In the depths of my soul, I knew that none of this was all right.

When I didn't answer him, the door closed again.

SEVENTEEN

ANNA WARD SAT at a small round table in the corner of the Stay Awhile tea rooms. The shop was busy, with groups of women and families enjoying an outing. The number of influenza masks had diminished over the past few weeks, as had the cases of the sick and dying. Summer was here, and it felt as if the world was finally turning a corner.

As I drew closer, I could see there was a thick white cup and saucer in front of her, and what looked to be a slice of Battenburg cake on a matching plate. She wore a dark green cardigan and sweater set, and her brown hair, liberally sprinkled with grey, was pulled back in a loose, untidy bun at her nape. She seemed so ordinary, this middle-aged woman who had been the catalyst for my life careering off the rails.

As if she had sensed me, Anna looked up and met my gaze. She didn't smile. I could see now that she hadn't slept well. There were dark shadows under her blue eyes and her skin had a sallow tinge, the flesh falling into unhealthy folds and lines as if she had lost weight abruptly.

"Mrs Flett," she said.

I drew closer. "Miss Ward." I noticed her empty cup as I sat down. "More tea?"

Anna nodded and I ordered for two from the waitress. The table next to us was served with some dainty sandwiches and I remembered I hadn't eaten this morning. Since the night we followed Owen, I hadn't eaten and barely slept. I had kept to the spare room as much as possible. Apart from frosty, unsmiling looks, Owen hadn't said anything more. Florence only came home long enough to check in on me. Aside from that, she was either working at the hospital—I was sure she had taken on some extra shifts—or staying at Eddie's. I was glad she was away from the situation, but I did miss her.

Owen had gone out again this morning, to the *Courier,* he said, but I didn't ask him to explain. If he was going back to that house in the East End, then there wasn't anything I could do to stop him. Even if I asked him for the truth, he would most likely lie, and if he told the truth it might only hurt worse. Things between us had deteriorated so quickly.

I had decided to go home to Belsham tomorrow. I told myself that was for the best, and my father would be happy to welcome me back. From the brief telephone conversation I'd had with him last week, he still wasn't enamoured with the girl from the village. I think the main problem was that she wasn't me.

How would I explain to him what was happening here in London? The quandary seemed insurmountable. After all the excitement of

Owen being alive, how was I going to tell him how horribly things had gone wrong?

The waitress brought the tea and we waited until she had bustled away. The group beside us was loud, but that was all to the good. I didn't wish for us to be overheard.

It seemed as if Anna wasn't going to open up the conversation, so I asked, "Why did you want to see me?"

She leaned closer, causing the table to wobble and the tea to spill over the tops of the cups and into the saucers. "To talk to you about your husband."

So did I, but I was prepared to allow her to go first. "If you read the story in the *Courier*, you must know all about it," I said. The story had caused such a stir that there had been other reporters ringing, all wanting to talk to us. So far, Owen hadn't agreed to anything, but I suspected it was only because of the book deal he and Sir Richard were negotiating.

"Your husband came back. You asked, and he came."

Anger and disappointment managed to creep into my voice. I believed I knew what she was getting at, and it infuriated me. "Coincidence," I said firmly. "He never died in the first place. Whatever price Dr McIvor charges for bringing back the dead, tell him I'm not paying."

Her gaze sharpened and she stared at me, as if reading my mind. The thought made me uncomfortable, though I told myself she could not possibly do so.

"Your husband has already spoken with Dr McIvor. Whatever payment was required has been discussed between them and paid."

I opened my mouth, but I had no words. The reason McIvor hadn't been in touch was because *Owen* had. The payment negotiated and made. But that would mean… I shook my head. It wasn't possible.

"Dr McIvor always chooses wealthy or important people to bring back. He says it is for the church, but I think…" She chewed her lip. "I believe he is not a good man, Mrs Flett, and I do not work for him willingly."

That did not surprise me. In fact, I could imagine Dr McIvor was more interested in lining his own pockets than the organisation he fronted.

After a beat, she straightened up. "I am here on a far more urgent matter," she said, and reached for her handbag, clicking it open and slipping her hand inside.

I thought she might be leaving, that she was reaching for her purse to pay, and I still needed to talk to her. I couldn't bear it anymore, and it was that desperation that forced the words from me.

"He's not my husband!"

She froze.

"I know how that sounds. Ridiculous and delusional. But he's not *Owen*. I understand that the war has changed so many men, and I should just be grateful that he's alive. But this isn't him, is it?"

Anna's eyes came alive. She licked her lips as if they were suddenly dry. "When your husband's spirit asked to speak to you, he was loud and insistent. In here." She tapped her temple. "I couldn't ignore him. Sometimes that happens. A very insistent spirit, desperate to make himself heard. When I tried to ask him what he wanted, he became too agitated to make himself understood, but there was something… He told me he had to stop you."

"Stop me from what?"

"From bringing him back."

I tried to speak, but my voice seemed to have dried up. "Why?"

She looked at me a moment more, then reached inside her handbag and took out a folded piece of newsprint. Her hand trembled. "I said that Dr McIvor has done this before," she said quietly. "That this isn't the first time he's brought someone back."

I looked to the paper. "What are you saying?"

Anna's face softened. "When he first found me, I was so humble and grateful. He thought I could help him with his mission. That was what he called it, his *mission*. The World Beyond is his idea, and he is very selective in the clients he chooses to help. I told myself they were special, that they should be grateful. He brought back their loved ones. Who would not want that?

She looked up at me. "Then I began to realise that such a thing is a curse, not a miracle. There are some things we are not meant to meddle with. It is beyond our realm. And when we do, we are punished."

I could see she believed what she was saying. That Dr McIvor had brought back my husband from the dead and now I was being punished for it.

"I don't believe you," I said, but my voice had lost its certainty. "Why would Dr McIvor choose me? I'm not rich or important."

"Your husband is. His story has captured the public's imagination. He's writing a book. He will share with others. The World Beyond will gain more follows. And that, I think, is more important to Dr McIvor than money. I think that was the price he asked."

I looked at my tea and saw that I had not even taken a sip. I reached for the cup but stopped myself. My hand was shaking badly.

Anna's next words were hurried. "When I came to Dr McIvor about my concerns, he said he had made adjustments. He said he had had years to refine his technique and nothing could go wrong. I tried to believe him, I *wanted* to. Then he said it was the war, and when so many die at once, that causes a problem. He said that he would fix it. But he hasn't."

I stared back at her.

"What we have done is very wrong," she said. "We are interfering in matters that we don't understand." She held out the slip of newsprint and I saw then she had a scar around her wrist. The same one as Owen.

I brushed it with my fingertips. "What is that?"

"It means I belong to Dr McIvor," she said. "He owns me, body and soul."

"He *owns* you?"

She held out the newspaper cutting again, and

when I didn't take it, set it down beside my saucer. Then she pushed her chair back and stood up, and without another word made her way through the maze of tables until I heard the bell on the door tinkle as it opened and closed behind her.

I then realised that I hadn't asked her about the image I had seen in the shop window. The Owen who had tried to speak to me, to warn me, about... something. But it seemed clear to me now. My Owen *had* come to me. He had been trying to tell me all along, through Anna Ward, and then in the window. He wanted me to be on my guard. Because the man who was living in his house and sleeping in his bed, who was sleeping with his wife, had never been Owen.

Owns me, body and soul.

I reached out, hand still shaking, and picked up the square of newspaper, unfolding it on the white tablecloth.

It was an article from one of the regional newspapers, and the year had been written in blue ink above the headline: 1916.

The war had still been raging.

CRUEL MURDER, screamed the headline.

```
   On    Saturday    evening,    Colonel
Peter   Martin   was   arrested   and
charged  with  the  murders  of  his
wife and two children.
   Colonel Martin had only recently
returned from the front, among much
celebration. Thought to be missing
in action, he had been found to be
alive and well.
```

> On Saturday, neighbours reported to the police that they hadn't seen the family for a few days and were worried. After other attempts to contact them failed, the police entered the home, where they found the bodies of Edna Martin, aged 29, and their two young girls, Helen (5) and Mary (7).
>
> Martin was found inside the house, alive but in a comatose and unresponsive state. He was transferred to St. Martin's hospital, where he remains under observation.
>
> So far, the police have found no motive for such a vile act. However, friends and family have said he hadn't been himself since his return. His wife had confided to her parents that she had grown afraid of him, and that he was no longer the same man.
>
> Due to his ongoing comatose state, an investigation will have to wait until…

My heart gave a dull thud. Was Anna telling me that Dr McIvor had brought this man back? That this was the inevitable result? One thing was for certain. Owen wasn't the same man. He wasn't my husband.

Who was he, though? *What* was he?

I stared at my cold cup of tea, the sounds of

light-hearted chatter swirling around me, feeling as if I was no longer part of this world.

What did Anna want me to do with this information? Go to the police? I could imagine the expression on Eddie's face. Although... perhaps he would not be so disbelieving, not when he had the evidence of what had happened to Florence. But the police were practical people. They looked at facts, and thus far I had few to go on.

Owen looked like Owen, therefore everyone believed he was Owen. Even if his behaviour was strange, it could be put down to his experiences during the war. Any doctor would say so. They would call me ungrateful.

I remembered that first night he came home, when I woke in the night and saw him sitting on the end of our bed in the light from the window. The strange look on his face. That sense of foreignness. As if he wasn't Owen at all. I hadn't listened to the warnings; I hadn't wanted to let anything negative spoil what had seemed a miraculous gift.

Tomorrow I would be returning home to Belsham, so if I was going to do anything then it had to be today.

The waitress had come back, a sympathetic look in her eyes. "Do you want that refreshed, love?"

I looked at the cold tea. "No. Thank you."

I dropped some money on the table. Outside, the bus stop was just ahead, but my steps slowed as I walked toward it.

The man in the newspaper had murdered his

wife and children, and Anna had suggested that it had happened before. And would happen again.

Did that mean this man, whoever he was, might do something so terrible to me? To Florence?

That was the question I needed an answer to: If this man wasn't Owen, then who was he? Because he had to be someone, didn't he? The man had a personality, character, and those didn't simply appear from the ether.

I tried to look logically at the things he'd sought to hide. The stolen knickknacks? I didn't think that was relevant. He had no connection to my father, for example, so why take the shepherdess statuette? Stealing seemed to be a symptom of a much bigger issue.

What about where he went in secret? A returned soldier would want to see his family, wouldn't he? He would want to pick up the ties to his past life. He might have parents, a wife. A girlfriend or lover.

I had assumed Owen was looking for excitement and pleasure when he took those trips in the Daimler. He was acting like a man who had never had a fast car like that. And what about the child Florence and I had seen run to him two nights ago in the East End? And the woman in the window. What if…?

I knew then what I had to do.

EIGHTEEN

THE TENEMENT LOOKED even worse in daylight. Shoeless children played in the street, their faces dirty and clothing ragged. There were a couple of women smoking cigarettes and gossiping, but I didn't want to approach them in case one of them was the person I was looking for. Instead, I found a man crouched down on his haunches by a wall, watching the world go by.

"I'm sorry to bother you," I said, anxious, and found his eyes on me behind a smooth mask. He was wearing one of the tin masks that had been given to soldiers whose faces had been disfigured in the war, and were considered too hideous to be out in public without being covered up.

"Got anything to help me out, missus?" he asked quietly, but he wasn't whining. He sounded angry, or resentful that he even had to ask.

I fumbled with my purse and found a pound note. "Of course."

He looked at it as if he'd like to refuse, and then snatched it out of my hand. He stood up and began to walk away, and I stumbled after him.

"Please. Wait. I wanted to ask you something."

He stopped, his back to me. Now the women were watching us, heads close together, eyes hard.

"I know someone who lives in that building." I nodded toward the tenement. "Not that well, mind you. We've only talked a couple of times. She's up the stairs, second room on the left. I want to help her, you see, but I don't want her to know. She wouldn't want my charity."

He turned to look at me, one of the eyes behind the mask cloudy white, the other dark and hard. I don't think he believed me, but there was always a chance he did.

"Please," I whispered.

He glanced up to the window. I remembered the two shadows before the gas light, merging together, before the blind came down.

"That's Bertha Robinson," he said. "Is that who you want?"

I committed the name to memory. "She's married, isn't she?" I asked, as if I wasn't sure.

He scoffed. "Was. Her husband died at Ypres. Not that he'll be missed. Right bastard, that one."

I must have looked shocked because he hesitated, unsure if he should say more.

"She's suffered a great deal," I said through stiff lips. "She's never said much about how he was killed. Was it an explosion? A German shell."

He made that scoffing noise again as he turned away. "Word of advice," he spat. "Don't waste your charity on Bertha."

I didn't even realise he had gone until I felt someone tug my sleeve. One of the children was standing, staring up at me, hair matted and dirty, nose a crusty mess. "Got a penny, lady?" she asked, holding out a grubby hand.

I fumbled in my purse again and found a penny. I heard one of the women call out.

"Your Maggie is out here again! Begging in the street. Should be ashamed of yourself, letting your child beg like that."

The two women shared looks, muttering their disapproval.

A moment later, a woman came running from the tenement doorway, straight toward us. I watched uneasily. She had a mass of dark hair and coal dark eyes, and although she had only stopped to pull on a coat over her flannel nightgown, she had added bright lipstick. When she saw the state of the child, she clicked her tongue impatiently and reached into her sleeve for a handkerchief.

"Maggie, what have I told you about going out looking like that?" she hissed, roughly wiping at the girl's nose.

"I was hungry," the child said with a sullen glance.

"You should have told me then."

"You was asleep."

The two of them exchanged a stare and then the woman clicked her tongue again, before she shot a look at me. "Kids, what can you do with 'em?"

"I haven't any," I said carefully, sensing an opportunity. "My husband died before we could start a family."

She nodded. "Mine's dead too. Bloody war." Something in her expression caught my attention, but it was gone too quickly for me to decide what it was. "What are you doing here? I heard there was a copper around here asking questions. You with the truancy people? Maggie here's been sick, so I haven't sent her to school."

I glanced at Maggie and realised she must be older than her height and build suggested. Poor diet probably.

"No, I'm not with anyone," I said quickly. "I was looking for a friend. We've lost touch." I almost said the name, but a sense of caution stopped me, or maybe the way the woman watched me with a smile that I didn't trust at all. I'd seen her look over my coat and shoes, and even though I did not consider my clothing expensive, it was a big step up when compared to the thin coat she was wearing.

"Lost touch, eh?" she repeated. "Maybe you're one of them do-gooders? My husband was always warning me about do-gooders. Might seem harmless enough, but they always want something in return. There's always a price to pay, that's what he said."

The words caught my attention. "That sounds like good advice. What was your husband's name?"

"Archie. Archie Robinson." I almost gasped. I'd suspected all along, but now I knew. This was Bertha, the very woman I was looking for. The woman Owen had visited last night.

She was attractive, despite the signs of hardship and poverty. Along with her dark hair and eyes, she had creamy skin and rounded cheeks, giving her a youthful look. I guessed she was older than she seemed. She put an awkward hand to her throat, and that was when I saw the bruises. They were fresh, and I could see the mark of each individual finger where someone had squeezed her.

Her eyes went hard and she hurried her little girl away from me without so much as a goodbye.

I should have demanded an explanation then. I should have confronted her. Told her that it was my husband who was with her last night. But I couldn't. I was like a frightened, injured animal, but instead of fight, all I wanted to do was run away and hide.

I turned and walked away. I didn't stop. I didn't stop until I reached the busy high street.

The journey home was a blur. I must have paid for my ticket and climbed aboard the right bus, then disembarked at my stop. I must have done all of that without causing comment, because the next thing I knew, I was in front of the house in Easton Street.

I didn't want to go inside, but I had little choice. Besides, I would be gone tomorrow, and it was a relief to let my thoughts rest on Belsham and the cottage and my father. I would be safe there, I told myself.

I was so caught up in my own head, I didn't notice the car parked outside, so I was surprised when I stepped inside and Florence and Eddie greeted me from the kitchen. They were seated at the table, teacups in front of them, their expressions serious. Florence looked pale and I could tell she had something to tell me.

"Emilia," she said. "I've told Eddie about us following Owen. About the woman we saw him with in that awful place."

Eddie glanced down at his cup, as though embarrassed.

"I asked Eddie to find out who she was," Florence went on.

I laughed then and sank down into the chair opposite. I must have sounded slightly unhinged because they stared at me. "Her name is Bertha Robinson, and her husband Archie died in the war. She's a widow."

Florence and Eddie exchanged a glance. "How…?"

"I've just been there. Do you think…?" I began. "I mean, perhaps Owen knew her husband? Perhaps he promised to watch out for them?" It was a plausible enough idea. I couldn't admit the truth to them. How could I explain to either of them what I really thought? What, deep inside me, I knew.

"It's worse than that," Florence said. "Tell her, Eddie."

He looked me in the eye, still uncomfortable with the situation. I suspected poking into a member of the public's private life wasn't something he should be doing. Not officially, anyway. "You're right. Her name is Bertha Robinson. She has lived at that address for five years and she has a child, a girl. Her husband died in Belgium in 1917. He was in Major Lanyard's company."

I knew that name! "I had a letter from Major Lanyard after Owen was killed. I kept it. It's at the cottage in Belsham. He knew Owen. I think they were friends. Does that mean that Owen knew Archie Robinson, too?"

I tried to imagine Owen consoling the widow of his friend. Even now, despite everything, I was still looking for a rational explanation, hoping that my wild suppositions regarding Anna Ward's confession were misplaced.

Florence shook her head. "Emilia, stop. There's more."

I looked again at Eddie and saw the pity in his eyes as he spoke.

"Yes, Owen and Major Lanyard were friends. It was the major he was going to see the morning he was killed. The reason Major Lanyard wasn't killed was that he was away from his bunker when the shell hit. He was busy with another matter."

"What other matter?"

"Archie Robinson was a deserter. That morning he was shot by firing squad. That's why Lanyard wasn't where Owen had arranged to meet him."

"A deserter?" I whispered. "But…"

Eddie continued on. "There were plenty of deserters. Men who were running from their own terrors as much as the enemy. Those who couldn't bear the pounding of the guns or the mud and horror one moment more. But Robinson wasn't one of those men."

"He wasn't?"

Eddie's mouth twisted with distaste. "He murdered a woman in a nearby village while on leave. He was seen by her son, and arrested. That was when he deserted. Lanyard decided to make an example of him, but no doubt was just glad to be rid of him. Before the murder, other incidents had come to light. Fights and thieving. Another soldier who was found dead after he reported Robinson for dealing in black market goods, though they could never prove he was behind that. Archie Robinson was a bad lot."

I heard Owen's voice in my head, as he crouched shaking in my father's house while Mr Stewart shot at the crows. *I didn't mean to do it.* Was he confessing to a murder?

"Owen's a journalist," I said tentatively. "Perhaps he was writing a story about Robinson. If they both knew Lanyard, then maybe—"

"Emilia," Florence took my hand in hers. "What we saw wasn't a journalist asking questions. You know it. They're lovers. But if we ask Owen what he was doing there, I'm sure he'll say something like that. He'll lie, just as he always does."

"He's visited her a few times now," Eddie added matter-of-factly. "Stayed overnight. I'm sorry."

"How do you know?"

"I sent one of my men to ask around. Discreetly."

The 'copper' that Bertha Robinson had mentioned. Then I remembered the bruises on her throat.

"Go home to Belsham," Florence said urgently.

"I don't know what's happening to Owen. I don't understand any of it, but you shouldn't be here. I'm going to stay with Eddie for a while... until we can sort this all out."

I nodded. I wanted to tell her about Anna Ward and Dr McIvor. Show her the newspaper article about Peter Martin. But I found myself unable to do either. They were still looking for a reasonable explanation to this madness—that Owen was living a sinister double life. And on the surface it did make sense. I had almost believed it myself.

But deep down, I knew the truth. Owen had never come back from the war. Archie had. And although at first Archie had tried his best to *be* Owen, that was no longer the case. He had either given up the pretence or he couldn't help himself. He was degenerating and he was dangerous.

I needed time to think. I needed time to consider all of this information before I could act.

NINETEEN

LETTER DATED 30 APRIL 1918

DEAR MRS FLETT,
My deepest and heartfelt sympathy on the loss of your husband, Captain Owen Flett. I do hope you will allow this intrusion into your grief by someone who, although he had not known Captain Flett long, knew him to be an honest and conscientious man.

At the time of his death, he had come to interview me about our incipient push into enemy territory during the long battle of Ypres. I had been called away on a matter of duty but was heading back to him when the shell struck the trench near my bunker. Unfortunately, Captain Flett and two of my men were caught in the blast. Although we were unable to recover their bodies, we know that they died instantly.

I wished to write to tell you how highly I thought of your husband. We had met a number of times at headquarters and I found him both honourable and courageous, and eager to write stories that would help those at home understand the life we soldiers were living. As you must know, he did not always obey instructions from his superiors and remain behind the lines, nor did he simply write that which others, both at home and abroad, wished him to, and I admired him all the more for that.

I remember on one occasion the conversation turned to our loved ones and he spoke of you in a way that made me believe he was longing to return to you. He told me that you were going to take a holiday together but had yet to decide where, although you were set against Siberia. It was a joke between you, I think.

I write this letter to you from my home in the Lake District, where I am recovering from wounds received in the line of duty. If you wish to write to me, I would be happy to receive a letter and to supply you with any further details, although I fear there is not much to tell.

Again, my deepest and sincerest sympathy on your loss.

Major Ernest Lanyard, Lakeside Cottage, Derwent Water

I spent a week with my father, soothing his ruffled feathers and proofreading the finished section of his next book. We talked about his characters and future research he might need me to do. Belsham hadn't changed at all, and it was like slipping on comfortable and familiar shoes.

We did not talk about Owen. Dad asked how he was and I said well. That was the full extent of the conversation about my husband. I think, if I had wanted him to, my father would have listened to me, though how much he would believe was another matter. But I didn't want to talk about Owen, and I knew my father was still disappointed that their reunion had fallen so flat. He must have sensed something was wrong, but he respected my wish to remain silent, for now at least.

When I told Dad I was travelling to see a friend in the Lake District, he sighed and rolled his eyes, but didn't complain too much. I think he was secretly glad I wasn't going back to London.

"Just a day or two," I assured him. "Then I'll be back."

He brightened. "I'll have the changes in the book done by then. You can read over them."

He hugged me goodbye at the station. He had never done that before. I felt guilty not having told him the truth, but how could I?

I'd reread the letter written by Major Lanyard. I'd kept it, among several other private memories, in a case under my bed. Mementos of my life with Owen, and his tragic death. It was bittersweet to look through them. Because the Owen I let into the house in Easton Street that night wasn't the same man. It was someone else masquerading as him. It was a reminder that my Owen was gone.

Now that I knew about Archie Robinson, I felt it was important I speak to the major. I had his address from his letter, and I needed to see him face to face. Robinson and Owen had died on the same day, around the same time, close to the same place. Was that somehow significant?

This was a puzzle that needed to be solved. Sometimes it felt as if I was so close, that I only needed a few more pieces and the truth would fall into place. But what then? I asked myself. Would that make everything all right? How could it?

The train shuffled along with an occasional blast of its whistle to warn people of its approach. I sat alone in my carriage, gazing out at the scenery. Misty hilltops and verdant valleys, lakes as smooth as glass that reflected back the cloudy skies. I had brought a book, but had yet to open it.

Lakeside Cottage was on Derwent Water, and the nearest town was Keswick. After I had reached the station, I found my accommodation, a small boarding house. The woman who owned it was nice enough, but extremely nosy. I didn't want to tell her my business, so I made up a story about needing some time to reflect. Once I had finished my supper, I was relieved to escape her and retire to my room.

I wondered how Florence was managing. She had called me before I left Belsham, ringing from Eddie's house, and seemed cheerful enough. It was only when I told her I was going to see Major Lanyard that she became concerned.

"What for? Emilia, I don't know what you hope to discover with all your sleuthing. You're starting to sound like a character in one of your father's novels!"

"It's the coincidence," I had explained. "It bothers me. Owen and Archie died in the same place at almost the same time. Doesn't it bother you, Florence? Don't you wonder what is happening?"

"Of course it bothers me," she said. "But I don't see any benefit in what you're doing. What difference does it make if Owen knew Archie Robinson or not? How will that change anything?"

I wasn't sure yet, but I knew it would.

"Have you seen Owen?" I asked casually, but she wasn't fooled.

"I went to get some of my clothes from Easton Street, and he was having a party," she said bluntly. "I wasn't going to tell you, but… I think you should know."

"What sort of party?"

"A loud and drunken one."

There was a silence between us for a time. I could hear her breathing.

"Who was there?" I was thinking of Bertha Robinson, though perhaps that was unlikely. I think he wished to keep his old life separate from the new.

"I saw Sir Richard through the window, so maybe it was to do with the *Courier*. Maybe they were celebrating that book deal he was talking about."

I wondered if McIvor owned Sir Richard too? *Body and soul*. I wasn't sure about anything anymore.

Florence was still speaking. "Honestly, Emilia? I don't know and I don't care."

But I could hear by her voice that she did care. She was hurt and confused, and she didn't know how to deal with this man who was not her brother. I suspected she was finding it easier to stay away from him than to see the changes in him.

I prayed my visit to Major Lanyard was justified. Florence may think I was wasting my time, but I believed the major could give me another piece of the puzzle. And just as Florence's way of dealing with things was to stay away and pretend it wasn't happening, I had come to terms with the fact that mine was to dig and dig, until I found answers.

Lakeside Cottage was five miles from Keswick. The weather was mostly fine, with only a sprinkling of rain, so I walked, enjoying the peace and quiet and beauty of the place. I saw the whitewashed structure through some trees, and the trickle of smoke from a chimney. A dog barked as I came to the door, and the man who answered was tall and gaunt. He was younger than I first thought, the lines and hollows in his face telling a story of pain and suffering, and he walked with a cane.

He looked at me expectantly.

"Major Lanyard?" I guessed.

"Yes. Well, I'm just Mr Lanyard these days."

"I'm Emilia Flett. You wrote to me last year about my husband, Owen. He was a correspondent for the *London Courier*."

His face brightened in recognition and he stepped back a little clumsily to let me in.

"Of course. Owen. I remember. Do come in, Mrs Flett."

By the time I had followed his slow, painful progress to a sitting area, he had remembered something else. "I read that Owen was alive. Bit of a miracle, that." There was a little frown between his brows. "Surely I wasn't mistaken?" His steady gaze was asking me why, if Owen was alive, I was here.

"No, you weren't mistaken," I said.

"But… is he with you?" He looked over my shoulder, as if expecting to see Owen in the doorway.

I smiled. "No. Only me."

He wanted to ask me why I was alone, but he was too gentlemanly and polite to do so. Instead, he insisted I sit down on the well worn sofa.

"Did you walk from Keswick? You're lucky you weren't drenched. My goodness." He went to find some tea to restore me. "My wife is normally here, but she's off visiting an aunt in Scotland. I had to almost forced her onto the train, she doesn't like to leave me alone. She thinks I can't cope."

The man was sweet, charming. He was so like Owen used to be that I could see why they had become friends.

"Mrs Flett, I don't mean to pry, but there must be a reason you've come all this way to see me." He leaned toward me, hands clasped between the knees of his flannel trousers. "I promise, I am a good listener."

I tried to smile, though not successfully. "You wrote me such a lovely letter and I wanted to thank you. I also wanted to ask you a little more about that time. You said if I ever wanted to, you would tell me more."

"I did, but that was before Owen returned to life," he joked, then frowned at something he saw in my face. "What it is?"

I hadn't known what I was going to tell him—the truth, or a subtle lie that covered most of the same concerns—but now that the time had come, the words spilled out of me.

"Owen isn't the same. I… I'm worried. I understand that men returning from war suffer both physically and mentally. My sister-in-law works in a hospital, so I do know. I don't expect him to be the same, but to be *so* different…"

"In what way is he different?" That frown was back between his brows. It had made a permanent line there.

I took a deep breath. "I'd like to ask you a question first," I said. "There was a man. Archie Robinson. He died the same day as Owen. Executed. Do you remember him?"

Lanyard looked away. I could see that the memory was not one he enjoyed, which was understandable. "Why do you want to know about Archie Robinson?"

"Owen has visited Robinson's widow. Several times. I think they are lovers."

He looked shocked. "Owen? Impossible! I like to tell myself that I am a good judge of character, and I would never have thought Owen was capable of such a thing. And with Robinson's widow!" He grimaced.

"He's changed," I said quietly. "Do you know if

he and Robinson were friends? I thought, if they were, his visits to the widow might make more sense."

But Lanyard shook his head. "Not at all. I don't think they even met. Owen wasn't there to see me about Robinson, either. He had asked me for an update on our actions and I was set to meet him regarding that, not deserters. The Robinson matter was somewhat last minute. I wanted it dealt with before the next big push. Robinson was a desperately unpleasant character if you want to know the truth."

"In what way?" I picked up my teacup and took a sip. It was too strong. Perhaps the major had got into the habit of drinking builder's tea in the trenches.

"The man was a liar, a thief and a murderer. He stole from his fellow soldiers, and he wasn't averse to selling stolen goods on the black market. The other chaps loathed him but sometimes they needed him, so most of the time they kept their feelings to themselves. It was later on, when he began to cross other lines, that they turned against him. A soldier in the same company died in mysterious circumstances and the finger was pointed at Robinson, although they couldn't prove anything. And then there was the murder of the woman, witnessed by her son. We arrested Robinson, he escaped, and once we recaptured him, his fate was sealed."

"He was shot?"

"It was my decision to do so that morning, before we went over the top. It wasn't pleasant, but war isn't pleasant. Sometimes I had to do things that still do not sit easily on my conscience. I suppose only my maker can decide whether I was justified in my actions."

"He was shot just before Owen was killed?"

"Yes. In fact, Owen probably saw the stretcher detail who were going to carry Robinson's body down to the hospital tent before the shell hit."

"So, if Owen didn't know Robinson, he couldn't have known Robinson's wife?"

"I can't see how, other than through wild coincidence."

There was silence between us as I finished my tea.

"I do remember something odd," Lanyard said. "I spoke to the men who survived the blast that hit Owen and the others. He was further back in the trench. His account of that moment mentions someone else, not in uniform, speaking with Owen just before the bomb hit. If I recall correctly, the man was calling out to Owen. I was never able to ascertain who that man was, and there was no record of him in the trenches any time before. I would have dismissed the matter if it weren't for one thing."

"What's that?"

"Another survivor on the opposite side of the blast saw him as well. And these two men had no chance to speak to one another before I talked to them. It puzzles me."

It puzzled me too. "Was it a colleague of Owen's?"

He shook his head. "The man had a full beard,

which is against regulations. I can only assume it was a soldier out of uniform for some reason. The thing is," and he looked at me apologetically, "if he hadn't detained your husband, he may well have escaped the blast unhurt."

I didn't know what to say. My throat closed up and I couldn't speak for a moment. Clumsily, I thanked him and gathered up my belongings. The major had answered my questions, it was time to go. And then he spoke again.

"The only thing Robinson regretted when he stood before the firing squad was that he was leaving behind his daughter." Lanyard shook his head. "He was what he was, a bad lot by any stretch of the imagination, but I suppose loving his daughter showed he had some humanity at least."

"His daughter?"

"He begged me to see that she was taken care of. Said he didn't trust his wife. I told him I'd do my best." With another shake of his head, he added, "I sent some money anonymously. A sop to my conscience, although the man had murdered at least two people."

It was like a puzzle I had been struggling to put together, and now that last piece had clicked into place. I stood up. "I should go."

He watched me with worried eyes. "Mrs Flett, I wish you well, I really do, but I sense you are holding something back. Owen… the Owen I knew was a man of integrity. He would always listen if spoken to honestly. Can you not speak of these matters to him?"

He didn't understand and I couldn't explain things to him. "I will try, Mr Lanyard. Thank you. I am most grateful for your time. I'm sure revisiting the past was painful for you, but I do appreciate it."

He stood up, reaching for his cane, but I moved quickly toward the door.

"There's no need, thank you. I will show myself out."

I walked a little way, the lake on my left, calm as a mirror. When I turned back, I could see him standing at the cottage gate, watching me. His gaze weighed heavily on me.

How could he possibly have understood what was in my mind? I hardly did myself. Because I believed that somehow Owen and Robinson had become entangled. Their souls? Their spirits? When Owen was returned to me he looked like my husband on the outside, but inside he was someone else. Inside he was Archie Robinson.

Was it just a terrible cosmic mix-up, or must there be a powerful reason for a dead man to want to live again? Why had Archie returned? What was so imperative that his soul would inhabit another man's body? It wasn't for his wife, the bruises on her neck proved that much. No, it must have been for his daughter.

TWENTY

AS SOON AS I turned the corner in the lane that led to my father's cottage, I saw it. The red Daimler. It stood out against the green hedge like a splash of fresh blood.

The journey back to Belsham had been interminable, despite having so much to think about. I was tired, too. I wanted to get home and sit with my father, soak in the peaceful atmosphere of the cottage while I decided what to do next.

I couldn't sit back and allow this version of Owen to run rampant. If he *was* Archie Robinson, as impossible as that seemed, then the news conveyed by Anna Ward's newspaper cutting meant at any moment he would begin to hurt the people around him. That man, Colonel Martin, had murdered his family. Was it only a matter of time before Owen did something similar?

I hadn't realised my steps had slowed until I stopped. The Daimler sat right outside of the cottage gate, its shiny red paint marred by a light splattering of mud. Owen must have driven up from London on the country roads.

And he was inside. With my father.

I quickened my steps, fumbling to open the

gate, and rushed to the door. I put my hand on the knob and stopped to listen. Not a sound. Heart pounding, I pushed open the door and stepped inside.

"Emilia?"

My father's voice came from his study. It sounded sharp, anxious, and I took a deep breath.

"Dad? Is Owen here?"

I was at the study door now, and I pushed it open.

My father was sitting at his desk, his eyes stark as they met mine, his hair on end. He looked as if he'd dressed in a hurry. His collar was askew, his face flushed. There were marks on his cheeks, as if someone had grabbed hold of his face and squeezed it. Hard.

"Dad?" I said into the stillness.

He cleared his throat and looked down at his desk. His papers weren't as neat as usual—several had scattered over the surface and fallen to the floor.

"Emilia."

I didn't jump, although it was a close thing. Owen was behind me, lounging against the wall. The casual pose was deceptive. His eyes and face were alert, while his hands at his sides twitched as if ready to strike.

"Where were you?" He watched me as if he were a hawk and I a field mouse.

"I was visiting a friend of my mother's," I said, the first thing that came to mind. "I told Dad, but he probably forgot."

I looked at my father and his eyes held mine,

as if he were trying to tell me something but was too afraid to speak. Perhaps it was just that Owen was dangerous. Of that, I already knew.

There was a squeak from the corner near the windows.

I turned my head and peered into the shadows. A familiar child was sitting on the floor, some of Dad's paper in front of her, a pencil clutched in her grubby hand. There were dried tears staining her cheeks, and she stared at me resentfully.

"Owen? Who is this?" I knew all too well who it was, but I wanted him to say it.

He walked away from the wall, throwing himself down into the armchair by the fire. I had so many memories of him in that chair, my father chatting with him, laughing or silent in contemplation. Companions. And now my father had bruises on his face.

"Maggie, say hello to Emilia."

The daughter he loved above all else. The daughter he didn't want to leave when he was shot for desertion. She was dirtier and even more dishevelled than she had been when I saw her with her mother. The neglect was obvious.

The little girl gave Owen a sullen look, as if she'd like to refuse, but I could see the fear in her eyes. "Hello," she mumbled.

"Hello Maggie."

I wondered if she recognised me, and then I wondered if she or her mother had told Owen about me.

"Owen," I moved closer, lowering my voice so the child couldn't hear. "What is she doing here?"

I could see he didn't want to answer, but he knew he had to.

"A friend of mine died in the war. A good friend," he said, doing his best to sound reasonable. "I told him I'd keep an eye on his family. I've been going over there… I could see his widow wasn't looking after their child, Maggie, not properly. That woman is an evil *slut*."

His self-control slipped for a moment, as anger resurfaced in him. I flinched, but he didn't seem to notice. His voice lowered, and I heard the determination in it, mixed with a hint of pleading. "I want to take care of Maggie. I want us to adopt her."

I didn't know what to say.

"Owen is being very kind, Emilia," my father said evenly. But having been raised by him, I knew when he was trying to humour someone, and when he was scared. "We should applaud him for it."

I nodded slowly, still looking at him. He wanted to protect me, and didn't want me to say anything that might set my husband off again.

"Want to go home," Maggie whined.

Owen shot her a look that was more helpless than irritated, and for a moment I wasn't as frightened of him as I had been when I first walked into the room. This man, this stranger, was worried about his child. He loved her, but he was out of his depth. He didn't know what to do about her, and he had brought her to me. He thought I would help him to care for her. He trusted me and thought that Maggie would be safe with me.

Surely I could use that to my advantage?

Maggie spoke up again, more determined this time, seeing that she had our attention. "I want to go home. Don't like it here."

Owen sighed again. "Well, you can't." He softened his voice with an effort. "You will like it here. You can play outside in the fresh air without getting sick. Perhaps you can go back to school?"

She shook her head stubbornly. "Don't want to." A tear ran down her cheek and her woebegone mouth trembled. Owen groaned and squeezed his eyes shut.

My father was still staring at me and when I caught his eyes, he mouthed something. *Florence. Phone.*

"I thought we could leave Maggie here. Just for now," Owen was saying. "While we make the proper arrangements."

"I don't want to be here," Maggie whined.

"Would you like something to eat?" I asked. Weren't children always hungry? "Or to drink? I think I have some humbugs in the pantry. Or do you like Jelly Babies?"

I had Maggie's attention now. She gave Owen a glance, and then climbed to her feet. "Do you have pink babies? I only like the pink ones."

"I think so. Shall we go and have a look?"

Owen was torn between coming to keep an eye on us, or staying to keep an eye on my father. We reached the door and I turned back to him with a smile. "We might need Owen to help us. The sweets are on the top shelf." It was enough to persuade him. He followed us to the kitchen.

The sweets weren't on the top shelf, but I pretended to scold my father for being so absent minded. Maggie giggled. I put the kettle on to boil to make a pot of tea, then dampened a cloth and began to wash Maggie's face while she was distracted with the Jelly Babies.

It was hard to call her a pretty child. There was something haunted in her expression, as if she had lived far more years than her age, and her dark eyes were too watchful to be innocent. None of that was her fault, of course. She had grown up in a world where only the robust and the lucky lived to old age. I wondered if her father had been the same.

I turned to Owen. His expression was softer than it had been in a while. If there had been any doubts left that this man was Archie and not Owen, they had now vanished. This look could only be given by a father to their daughter.

I was so involved in my thoughts that it was a moment before I heard the front door open, followed by the thud of boots on the floor. Maggie stumbled back, her thin face wary, and Owen caught her.

"Owen Flett?"

A police constable, middle-aged and burly with a bristling moustache, marched into the room. He could have been a character in one of my father's novels as he stepped forward from the shadows into the kitchen.

"Owen Flett, I am arresting you for assault and kidnap."

Owen was already on the move, turning to

the back door, Maggie's arm in his hand. But his flight was anticipated. Another policeman was outside the door, and between the two of them, Owen was overpowered.

I saw fear in his eyes before it was hidden behind his bravado. "Shouldn't you be arresting Bertha? For neglect? There are bruises all over that child. What sort of mother does that?"

The constable responded in a calm voice. "If what you say is true, then I'm sure it'll be investigated. Come along, now, Mr Flett."

"Where are you taking him?" I asked. My father was standing in the passage, hanging back a little, his face pale.

"Down to the local station," the constable answered.

"What about Maggie?" Owen asked frantically.

"We have instructions to hold you for some bigwig from London. They said the girl could stay here till he arrives."

"I can't just leave her for Emilia to look after." But the look in his eyes was begging me to do just that.

"She'll be safe," I said. "I promise."

He hesitated a moment more, then he was manhandled toward the door. I didn't follow.

I took a deep breath, and then another one. My hands were trembling, and I felt a bit light headed. Some bigwig from London? Could it be Eddie? It might explain why they were told to leave the girl here in the meantime. I had so many questions.

But answers could wait. I was safe. *We* were safe.

I kept thinking about the newspaper clipping of Peter Martin. How Owen seemed to have trouble controlling himself. My father was shaken up, but matters could have been far, far worse.

I made the tea and my father and I, and Maggie, went into the sitting room.

"Florence rang just before he got here," my father said in a low voice, eyes on the little girl, who was busily sucking on her sweets. She had several laid out before her, in order of preference, and was working her way through them.

"She was looking for you. She said Eddie—is that her man's name?—was worried. I told her you were still away and then Owen's car pulled up outside. I saw him through the window coming to the front door with the little girl. She told me to be careful and that she would have Eddie get someone over here in ten minutes. Unfortunately, it took longer than that."

"Did he hurt you?"

He didn't want to tell me the truth. He still thought of Owen as Owen, and believed I would be upset. I *was* upset, but not for the reasons he thought.

"I'm not easily frightened, Emilia, but he frightened me. I didn't know what he intended to do. That's not something I ever thought I would say about Owen."

I reached to take his hand in mine. "We can't think about him as Owen, not anymore. He's dangerous, you're right, and we have to protect ourselves."

Maggie chose that moment to look up from her sweet sorting. "I want to go home now," she said.

TWENTY-ONE

FLORENCE SLIPPED HER arm around my shoulders, trying to comfort me. I was glad I was sitting down because my knees wobbled. I leaned against her, feeling exhausted.

We were back in Easton Street. After Eddie and Florence arrived in Belsham, Eddie had gone to the local police station and taken charge of Owen. They were going to drive him back to London, where he would be charged and held until brought before a magistrate.

Florence and I returned to London in the Daimler, and by the time we arrived home, we realised how much of an emotional toll the situation had taken on both of us.

I didn't want to leave my father, but he insisted he was all right. As for Maggie, arrangements were made for her to be taken into care until a relative could assume charge of her. Her mother was in hospital. That was when I learned that Owen had beaten her, which was bad enough, but it might have been worse had a neighbour not intervened. She might have died.

Florence helped me into a chair. "That isn't Owen, is it?" she said, hovering over me. "I've tried to tell myself that he has changed because of the war, but I just… He is so different, Emilia. As insane as it seems, I keep thinking he was never Owen to begin with. It isn't just that his personality has changed, or he forgets things… He's like a stranger play-acting at being Owen."

It was well past time I shared my beliefs with her, impossible as they were. "There's something I need to tell you."

Florence took a breath. "I think we both need a brandy first," she said, and went to pour it.

When we'd taken a good gulp of the fiery liquid, I told her everything. From my return visit to Dr McIvor, to Owen coming home, and all the differences I had seen in him. My fears about this stranger with my husband's face. Anna Ward's warning, the newspaper clipping, Major Lanyard's description of Archie Robinson, and the connection to the woman we had caught Owen visiting in the East End. Florence listened, interrupting with questions. So many questions.

"How could McIvor change Owen for Archie? And why?"

"I don't know, but I'm going to find out."

"Does everyone he brings back in another body go insane?"

"Anna Ward said McIvor told her he had fixed the problem. But he hasn't. I think Colonel Peters is only the tip of the iceberg."

"Owen…Archie might have killed you and your father."

"Yes. Prison is the only safe place for him."

Florence was still trying to wrap her head

around the impossible when we heard Eddie return.

"Don't tell Eddie," she said quickly. "I need to think all of this over. I still don't…" She took a sharp breath. "You know, I *believe* you, Emilia, but I don't think Eddie will be able to. This may be too much of a stretch for him."

I agreed.

Eddie came into the room and Florence went to embrace him. He looked surprised, and then hugged her back. "Your brother is being looked after," he assured her. "I don't know why he did what he did. The story he's telling… doesn't feel right. Perhaps he really was trying to help that child, but I wish he'd come to me first."

"What will happen to Maggie?" I asked.

"She's staying in care while we question her mother. Owen was right, the child is covered in bruises."

I felt sick at the thought. "Her mother?"

"She claims that Owen punched her, and it was he who bruised the child. There's evidence from the neighbour, too, but I think it will be exceedingly difficult for him to claim he is innocent." He looked from Florence to me. "I think you should both prepare yourselves for the worst."

"Thank you," I murmured.

"There is more, if you're up to it."

Florence nodded.

"Archie Robinson. He had a long list of charges against him before the war. Spent some time in jail, too. After his last offence, he was given the choice of returning to jail or joining the army. Unfortunately, the army didn't seem to have changed him for the better. There were more charges to add to the rest, some proven and others only suspected. They believe he murdered two people. He was shot for desertion."

We already knew that, unbeknownst to Eddie. Florence made the right sounds, trying not to meet my eyes. I saw Eddie reach into his jacket pocket and take out a photograph. He set it down on the table between us.

"This is Robinson. I wondered if either of you had ever seen him or a photo of him before? I'm still trying to understand how Owen knew Mrs Robinson, or how he became involved in this mess."

I looked down at the photograph. Archie Robinson stood in front of a waterfall and trees, the sort of painted backdrop photographers kept in their studios. He was lean with broad shoulders, his dark hair was combed back, his face interesting rather than handsome. I didn't recognise him, and then I did. Something about his loose, reckless smile, the gleam in his eyes. As if he was up for anything, as if nothing could scare him.

The Owen who had come back from the dead… I recognised that look in him. "No," Florence said for both of us. She glanced at me and I wondered if she had noticed the resemblance too. The sense that this man lived in her brother's body.

Eddie slipped the photo back into his jacket.

"Can we see Owen?" I asked him.

"Of course. Wait until tomorrow, though. I think he might be calmer then."

I wondered what Owen had been saying but didn't ask. I nodded. "Thank you, Eddie. I... this has been an awful time for everyone and you have been nothing but understanding."

He nodded. "There'll be worse to come," he warned, "but I'll help you through as best I can."

If Eddie had his way, I knew Owen would go to prison. Archie deserved to be punished, but what of *my* Owen? If Archie had taken Owen's body, where was Owen now?

Florence and I were too tired to talk. Almost too tired to think. I changed the sheets on the bed that Archie and I had shared, ridding myself of the smell of him, if not the memories. I felt wretched. I had slept with another man, and the worst of it was, I had enjoyed it.

I tossed and turned for a long time and eventually fell into a restless doze.

I became aware of the soft brush of fingers against my face. I wanted to open my eyes but my lids were too heavy. I was in that place that was neither asleep nor awake.

"Emilia," a beloved voice whispered. "Listen to me."

I didn't care if this was a dream, it felt very real. I wanted it to be real. "Owen."

"Listen to me. I am between worlds, in limbo.

I am suspended in a place that is neither heaven nor hell."

"I wanted you back!" I wasn't sure if I spoke the words aloud, but he heard them anyway.

"I know you did. It wasn't safe. I tried to tell you."

"Owen," I groaned. "This is my fault. I should never have—"

"No!" He sounded as if he was trying to convince me and I struggled to open my eyes but they were still too heavy.

"What will happen to you?"

"I will stay here until my body is freed of the soul inside it. Until then I cannot be at peace."

I thought of Archie, the ultimate survivor. He might be in prison now but he would get out, he would go somewhere else and continue with his life, perhaps for *years.*

"Can you…can you come back? Like Archie did?"

I heard the tremulous hope in my voice and held my breath for his answer.

"Emilia," he whispered, and I felt his cold lips brush mine. "I am dead. The dead don't come back."

I sat up in the bed with my eyes wide open.

All around me was darkness and silence. Owen was gone.

Had it been a dream? I was no longer sure, but there was one thing I did know. I would not risk leaving Owen in such a place, abandoned in purgatory. I needed answers, and there was only one person I could ask.

"Mrs Flett? Miss Flett?"

Dr McIvor looked surprised to see me and Florence back in Tottenham Court Road. And wary. I could not mistake the flash of suspicion in his eyes. "You must be very glad your husband is home. If you are here regarding payment, you may rest easy. I have already settled that with him."

I glared at him. "*Owen* didn't come home."

His smile faded a little, but didn't disappear. "I beg your pardon?" He acted as if there was nothing odd about the whole affair. As if he brought dead men back to the world of the living all the time.

Florence's voice was low and angry. "The man who came home isn't Owen. And you know that."

Before he could dispute what she'd said, I jumped in. "You made a mistake, and I think this has happened to you before, Dr McIvor."

The smile was gone now.

"May we come in?" I asked politely. "Or should I ask our friend from Scotland Yard to join us?"

Despite my warning, we hadn't told Eddie what we were doing. It was just the two of us.

After a moment of hesitation, McIvor widened the door and stepped back. "Come through." He led me into the sitting room. That was when I saw Anna, her hair untidy, her face pale and anxious.

McIvor shot her an angry look. "You told her."

Instead of cowering, Anna raised her chin. "She needed to know," she said. "After what's happened before, she had to be told so that she could protect herself. I refuse to have another death on my conscience."

"That was a mistake," McIvor hissed. "I told you, I've fixed it."

"But you haven't." Her voice was shaking now. "This is dangerous, Dr McIvor. You have no right to play God."

He clenched his hands into fists at his sides. "If it weren't for me, you would still be sitting in your mother's shabby parlour! What was the most exciting thing that happened there? Tedious spirits with their tedious problems." He imitated one of the voices, mocking her. "'Ask Father where he put his pocket watch?' Your talents were wasted, Anna. I *saved* you, gave you a place in my church, gave you true purpose. Don't tell me you want your mediocrity back again, because I won't believe you."

"At least my conscience was clear! I did not have to worry that the next person who came to my seance might die at the hands of a loved one!"

"Do you really think any of those people would have refused me? They *begged* me! I can take my pick of the souls on offer and the more I have, the more I understand. This war is an opportunity that may not come again."

I felt as if the floor tilted beneath my feet. His pick of souls? What did he mean by that, exactly?

Anna wasn't finished yet. "You told me it would not happen again and then Colonel Martin killed his wife and children. And there have been others. You know it's true. You said you had 'fixed it' then but you haven't. You know it, yet you refuse to admit it."

He waved a hand. "The benefits far outweigh the costs."

"Whose benefits? Yours? Certainly not theirs!"

McIvor's answer was dismissive. "Anna, you see so much, and yet understand so little."

I had heard enough. Everything I'd feared was true. I stepped between them and Anna stumbled back, while McIvor turned his face to me. His eyes were black pits of rage. He was frightening, but I refused to let him intimidate me. All the same I was very glad to feel Florence's hand on my shoulder.

"Tell me what happened to Owen! Tell me how you could make such a terrible mistake?"

Slowly, the anger in the doctor's face drained until he was almost as pale as Anna. "It is not an exact science, bringing souls back, and when two people die very close to each other in time and place…"

"The wrong soul returns in the wrong body." It made a terrible sense. In war, many people died at the same time, and in the same place. "Where is Owen's soul, then? He said…" I swallowed. Should I tell McIvor what Owen had told me? I hadn't told Florence yet so I decided not to. "Where is he now?"

McIvor's expression turned watchful. "Neither in the living world nor in the world of the dead."

"Purgatory," Anna answered for him.

It was true then. My heart broke as Florence' hand tightened, and I heard again Owen's whisper.

I am dead. The dead don't come back.

I didn't believe that was the end of it. I wouldn't! Archie had come back, why not Owen?

The doctor didn't look happy as he spoke to Anna. "If you wish to call it that. It is not a word I like to—"

"Can you still bring him back? Bring my husband back and leave Archie in his place?"

"Emilia," Florence murmured, as if in warning. At the same time I heard Anna catch her breath, heard her whisper to the doctor, "Can you do that?"

McIvor opened his mouth, but I spoke first. "Why can't you? You brought Archie Robinson here. Why can't you send him back? I want Owen, the real Owen."

"It's too dangerous," McIvor said through stiff lips. "I have never tried to return a soul, let alone switch one for another. I don't know if it can be done. I don't know what the consequences will be if I fail."

"The consequences to Owen?" Florence asked. She looked at me, and I knew what she was thinking. Could things be any worse than they were now? "Do you think Owen would want to take this chance?" she asked me. "This risk?"

"To be alive again, here with us?" The thought of Archie living on, using Owen's body, while Owen floated in darkness... This was my fault and I couldn't bear it, and I didn't think Owen could bear it either. "I think we should do whatever we need to, if there is a chance."

I turned in time to see the light in McIvor's dark eyes. A glimmer of interest. As if we were all experiments to him rather than human beings. "I suppose it's possible," he mused. "Someone will have to make the journey." He smiled with satisfaction. "It was you who asked for him to be returned, Mrs Flett. If you hadn't done that then we would not be in this position, would we? His soul could have moved on instead of being trapped in another man's body. Are you willing to travel into that dark place, that gap between worlds, to find him?"

"Yes." I didn't even have to think about it. "You're right. This is my fault. He's lost because of me. I have to find him, I have to—"

"Emilia!" Florence had tears in her eyes. She turned to McIvor. "What will happen if this fails?"

The doctor spoke in his usual pragmatic manner. "There are no guarantees she will return at all. I will tether her soul to me, but she may still be trapped in that dark place forever. You and your husband, together, Mrs Flett, and yet as distant as planets circling the sun."

I felt as if a shadow fell over my soul. And then I thought of a life lived without Owen, while Robinson stood in his shoes. "I don't care," I whispered. "I want to try. I *need* to try."

McIvor stroked his chin. "I need time to think. And I will need the body." Then, to me, his voice sharper. "Where is he now? Your husband?"

"If you mean Archie, then he is in jail."

McIvor sighed. "It won't work without his consent." He now sounded sceptical. "Is it even possible to gain his consent? A man like that, a deserter who has nothing to gain by agreeing?"

So he *did* know about Archie.

But there was something *I* knew Archie Robinson would do anything to keep safe. Even if it meant agreeing to go back to the gap between worlds.

There was a knock on the door, startling us. Anna's eyes widened. "That will be our next client," she whispered. "I don't think I can perform right now."

McIvor gave her a scornful look. "You will do as you are told. I will let them in."

As soon as he was out of earshot, Anna turned to me. "Don't trust him," she said. "Once he has bound you to him, then you will be his."

I didn't understand what she meant but I knew she was right, McIvor was not to be trusted. But if I had the slightest chance of making right this terrible wrong, and saving Owen, then I knew that I had to try.

TWENTY-TWO

THE MAN WHO wasn't Owen leaned forward, his hands clasped between his spread knees, eyes on the floor. He looked up as soon as he heard Eddie's voice at the barred window of the metal door. And when he saw me, his eyes narrowed.

"Emilia," he began, with a hint of wariness. He stood up and came to the window. "Maggie…?"

"She's being cared for," Eddie said before I could answer. "We're investigating her mother. You know it would have been better if you had come to me before you acted on your own account?"

Owen shrugged. "I was angry. I have a short fuse and a hot temper."

The Owen I loved had had neither. His grey eyes, those familiar eyes, now shifted to me.

"Can I speak to Owen alone?" I asked, without breaking contact.

Reluctantly, Eddie agreed and moved away, stopping near the stairs that led up to the police station. These cells were for prisoners awaiting release or, in Owen's case, a magistrate's decision. Eddie had already told me that it was unlikely my husband would be let out on bail but would instead be transferred to one of the larger prisons. He had assumed neither Florence nor I would want to pay to have him bailed into our custody, even if such a thing were possible.

As soon as we were alone, with only the metal bars between us, Owen smirked. It was a travesty of the smiles he used to give me. "What do you want to know?"

"I want my husband back, *Archie*," I retorted, my throat aching. "And you're going to help me."

He gave a low chuckle. "Good luck with that. I'm not even sure what I did to deserve getting here. Dying at exactly the right time, I was told. Shot by firing squad and then getting a second chance." He laughed softly. "But as long as I *am* here, I'm staying. I'll swear to everyone who asks that I am Owen Flett, and you are my loving wife. I'll say you have a mental problem. Awfully sad." He pulled a clown face to mock me. "I've tried to keep it quiet, but now it's obvious you're getting worse, so what can I do? Maybe you need treatment? A few weeks locked up in a nut house, perhaps? Maybe months?" He chuckled.

I tried to still the flare of unease in my stomach. I didn't think for a moment this man was bluffing. He would fight tooth and nail to stop me from sending him back, and was willing to fight dirty. He had no sense of right or wrong, no conscience. But I would fight too, and harder.

"Florence knows about you too," I said.

"Ah, my poor little sister. *Very* unstable. I doubt she'll be believed any more than you. Come on,

Emmy, who would believe that Owen Flett has returned from the dead, only it's not really Owen at all." He lifted his voice in an imitation of mine, "*There's another man in Owen's body!* Honestly, it sounds like something written by Edgar Allen Poe."

I was quiet for a moment, watching him laugh silently to himself, so certain that he was going to win this battle. He thought he would remain here, live the life of Owen, spend his money and play his part, and I would be helpless to stop him.

"How did you know about Owen, about his life? You very cleverly pretended to have amnesia about some things, but you knew so much."

"Our friend Dr McIvor filled me in on what he could, and the rest… When people think you're a certain person, you pick up bits and pieces. I have Owen's face, his body, his voice. I seem to have some of his nuances." He grinned at the word. "See, like that! When I was me I would never have known a word like *nuances*. If I concentrate hard enough I can access Owen's memories, like reading a book. Not always though. It's a book with pages missing."

It explained so much.

He leaned closer, his expression hard and determined. "The thing is, *wife*, I like being Owen."

"What does McIvor get out of this?" I asked him.

He grinned. "The question you really have to ask is, what does McIvor get out of them. The people he supposedly saves to benefit his shonky church."

"Supposedly?"

"Ask yourself, if you push a child in front of a bus and then pull them away before it hits—have you actually saved its life?"

I was confused by Archie's words.

"What if I were to tell you that Owen only died because McIvor *wanted* him to? And only because he planned on bringing him back."

He looked at me conspiratorially, as if he had just laid the truth bare before me. "But your *honourable* husband refused to play the game. Not me though. So McIvor was stuck with me, and he had to make the best of it."

One part stood out from the rest and I felt a chill all the way to my toes. "Wanted him to die?" I whispered. "But…Owen died when a shell exploded."

Archie winked. "Ah, but the good doctor made sure he was in the right place at the right time."

Major Lanyard had said there was a strange looking man in the trench. A man who detained Owen.

Otherwise, he may well have escaped the blast unhurt.

Could that have been McIvor? Did he have the sort of power that allowed him to do such a thing? I struggled to believe it, but then I asked myself why not. McIvor could transfer another soul into Owen's body and bring him back from the dead. Why not facilitate his death, if it suited his needs? A man like Owen, a respected journalist, espousing the wonders of McIvor's church, would be tremendously beneficial.

It was time I saved Owen, *my* Owen, from McIvor's twisted machinations.

Eddie was still over by the stairs, talking quietly with another policeman, well out of hearing distance. He saw my glance and moved toward me, but I held up a hand and shook my head. He stopped and went back to his conversation. Good, that was good. When I turned back to Owen, something in my expression must have warned him. He went very still.

"What are you plotting, Emilia?" he said. "You know you can't win. I'm thinking we can come to some arrangement. I'll stay out of your way and you can stay out of mine."

"No. I'm going to send you back," I told him. "I'm going to find my husband and bring him home."

He chuckled, but there was that wariness in his eyes. "And how do you intend to do that? Do you have a time machine?"

"I don't need one. I am going to the underworld, and you're coming with me."

He snorted a laugh. "Nonsense. You can't do that."

"I can, and I will."

I saw it then, the soul of the man who had stolen my husband's body, and it was dark and dangerous. I was glad of the bars between us because he looked capable of anything at that moment.

"You had your chance of life," I said, leaning forward.

"Yeah? He had his chance too."

"But if what you say is true, then his life was stolen from him. McIvor cheated."

He sneered. "Cheated? You say that as if you think life is fair, Emilia. Trust me, it's not."

"No, you're right, life isn't fair. But I suspect there is a balance to it. And what McIvor has done can only have disrupted that balance. You were never meant to be here, Archie. You need to go back, and I'm taking you."

"You'll fail," he replied through gritted teeth.

I smiled. "I won't. Because you're going to help me. And do you know why?"

He snorted. "Why?"

"Because of Maggie."

All at once, the bravado went out of him. "What do you mean?"

"If you want your daughter to live a good life, a *safe* life, then you will help me. Isn't that what you want, Archie? You saved Maggie from your wife and brought her to me, because you know I can look after her, and I *will*.

"At the moment she's in the care of some nameless government department, waiting to see if there's a relative somewhere who can take her, although I doubt she will ever be loved. Or perhaps she will be returned to her mother only to be hurt again. Bertha blamed you for Maggie's bruises, you know. And given where you are right now, who are they more likely to believe?

"More bruises, Archie. Cringing in terror at what might happen today or tomorrow or in a year. Do you want that? I'm offering your daughter a chance to have a life where she's loved and cared for. I'll send her to school and watch over her. I promise you that, and you know I will keep my promise."

He stared at me, his mouth slightly ajar, eyes fixed on my face. "You'd do that?" he said.

"You know I would. But if that doesn't convince you, then think on this. McIvor might believe he's a genius, but he's made mistakes. The souls he has placed in the wrong bodies aren't comfortable. They lose their minds. Anna Ward told me there have been murders. Men, who McIvor brought back, who turned on their loved ones and killed them. You might think that won't happen to you but can you be sure? That you won't turn on Maggie and snuff out her precious life?"

He looked pale now. He must have felt that instability inside him. Perhaps one of the reasons he had brought Maggie to me was because he didn't trust himself. It was established he was abusive even before he died and now the situation was so much worse.

I removed the papers from my handbag. I had a solicitor draw them up. "I have the legal documents here. All you have to do is sign them. But only if you willingly come with me. You cannot refuse once we start our journey. You cannot run away. If you do, then Maggie is lost. Do you understand?"

There was a long moment between us, but finally he nodded. His head fell as if there was no strength left in him. I couldn't trust him completely, but I believed he would go through with this for the sake of the daughter he loved. Possibly the only thing in his life that he *did* love.

"Will you do it? Will you come with me to the underworld? Will you do what I ask of you?"

McIvor said it was important that he verbally agree to this. I needed to hear him say the words.

"Yes. I will." Now he did look at me and there was loathing in his eyes. He hated me, but that didn't matter.

I turned and waved Eddie over. "I need to arrange bail," I said.

Eddie looked at me as if I had lost my mind. But before he could try to persuade me against it, I held up my hand.

"I mean it, Eddie. Florence knows, and we are in agreement on this. We want Owen home."

I'd lost his respect, I could see that in his expression before his face became that of a policeman again, but it didn't matter. It was too late to turn back, there was only forward. And whatever awaited me.

TWENTY-THREE

THE SILENCE IN the room was like a weight upon my shoulders. I was seated in front of Anna Ward, our chairs facing each other. She held my hands, her skin soft and cool while mine was hot and damp. I was sick with fear and desperation. I wanted to wipe the perspiration off, but I couldn't break contact with the medium. I'd been warned several times what would happen if I did.

I heard a shuffle behind me on the sofa. Archie was there, handcuffed. So far he was compliant, but dangerous nonetheless. Florence watched him like a hawk, her worried gaze going from him to me and back again. She knew her brother was another man, but I wasn't sure she believed what we were attempting was even possible. But *I* believed it, and for now that was enough. As for Eddie, she would have to bring him around afterwards.

There was a scar about my wrist, just like Archie's. Before taking my place with Anna, McIvor had gripped my hand to prepare me for my journey. I saw his tattoo properly for the first time then. What I had thought was a man's face was in fact far more demonic. Ugly inhuman features and sharp teeth, with tendrils of vines erupting from its mouth. As he held me, the image seemed to crawl toward my hand, and there was a sharp pain. As though something had bitten into my flesh.

I was now tethered to him, body and soul.

McIvor had also instructed me at length on what I must do. With Anna's help, Archie and I would go to 'the gap between worlds' together. Once there, Archie would be taken to his final destination, and I could bring Owen back with me.

"Only you can make the journey home, you will have no help from Anna or myself, but your tether will lead you. On the way you will pass through a number of realms, and the final one of these will be the realm of dreams. When you reach that you will know you are close. But, and this is most important, during your journey you must not turn back to look at Owen. Not even once. Not even a glance. If you do, then all your efforts will be wasted and he will be flung back into the realm of lost souls. Do you understand, Mrs Flett?"

His dark eyes were ablaze with excitement, and he licked his lips as if he could taste my fright. He was enjoying himself far too much, and I caught Anna staring at him with concern.

At last, it was time to begin. Anna's soothing voice washed over me, filling the silence of the room and stilling my frightened thoughts. "Breathe slowly, Emilia. Let yourself drift. The world is no longer beneath your feet. You are floating above it, drifting. Think of Owen. He is waiting for you. He will find you. He will show you the way."

For a time, I thought I was sleeping, only it wasn't truly sleep. Then I realised that I was walking in a frightening landscape unknown to me, yet also familiar.

I had seen photographs of the war. Everyone had. The devastation it had brought to the fields and villages and whole countries. I had never seen it with my own eyes, however, until now.

Soil was piled up on a bare landscape. Hollows led down into a mess of dark water and broken things—human and animal. I was walking through No Man's Land, and I saw the remains of a trench in front of me. Only this wasn't actually what it was. It was my mind's way of interpreting what I saw. McIvor had said that seeing this world as it truly was would drive the living mad, so my brain made sense of the impossible by applying known images to what lay before me.

"He's here."

The voice brought my head around, and I saw Anna standing behind me in her brown skirt and white blouse, and her warm slippers. It was strange to see her ordinariness in this horrific landscape.

Beside her, his hand in hers, was the true form of Archie Robinson. I recognised him from the photograph Eddie had shown me, but this man's shoulders were slumped, his head was bowed, and all of his reckless smiles were gone.

Anna looked at something beyond me, and

when I turned back, I saw Owen standing by the wreckage of a wooden barricade. He still wore his army uniform and his satchel was over his shoulder, no doubt full of his notebooks and pencils, and the photo of me he kept with him. He must have looked like that on the day in 1917 when the enemy shell took his life. When McIvor took his life.

I was still staring at him when I felt a larger hand slip into mine. Archie was now beside me. He was looking at Owen too, his expression both jealous and resentful. Then his gaze moved over our surroundings and he swallowed.

"Good luck, Emilia. Remember, follow the tether and do not be distracted. I will be waiting for you and Owen." Anna's voice was already beginning to fade. She could not help me on this next part of the journey.

What had passed for daylight here was also fading, and the world seemed to get darker and darker.

"Emilia."

Owen was calling to me, only he was further away now.

"Wait!" I cried out, my heart thumping. I could feel the chair beneath me and Anna clasping my fingers in hers, yet I could not see her. I could only see Owen.

Although he was a pale, washed-out version of the vibrant man I loved, it was truly him. Smiling at me.

"Owen," I breathed.

"Come on!" I remembered him saying the

words in just that way so many times before. *Come on* as we walked across the fields at Belsham, *come on* as we hurried for a train, *come on* as he tugged me upstairs to our bed.

He turned away and took a few steps, then looked over his shoulder at me. I went toward him, barely noticing Archie at my side. It was so dark now and whatever path we were on was rough. Above me, the sky was an opaque black, pressing down. We were still in No Man's Land and I could smell damp and the scent of bonfires drifting up from somewhere below. Owen seemed to have a faint light of his own in the darkness.

Archie made a sound and I glanced back at him and even in the gloom, I could see the terror in his eyes. "This place," he said. "I remember this place."

Was he going to change his mind?

"Think of Maggie. You have to do this for Maggie." I squeezed his hand. "I'm here for her. I will be there for her."

He stared at me with wild eyes, but I must have got through to him because his hand relaxed on mine.

When I turned back, Owen was gone. Disorientated, I tried to stay on my feet, shocked and very afraid.

Archie was pointing ahead. "The station is down there."

"Station?"

"That was where I went when I died. A place where soldiers made their last journey by train. I don't know…perhaps it isn't really like that, but that's what I saw."

A station would be familiar to him. It made sense he would see Hades like that.

It wasn't pitch dark after all. There were murky lights coming from somewhere in front of us. We started off again, our shoes crunching on hard ground, the rattle of stones.

A moment later, we were on a decaying platform.

Walls were broken and falling in, stone was crumbling. The place was in ruins. I could see the tracks used by the trains, but other than that the station could have been abandoned. I wondered what would happen once the tracks were gone too. If Owen was still here would he be forever trapped in the gap between worlds?

I had come to save him, to bring him home, but as I looked about me at the awful place I told myself that getting him out of limbo would be enough. Giving him the chance to move on, wherever that was.

There was a puff of steam and I realised a train had arrived further down the ruined platform. There was no one waiting to board it. When I turned back I saw a shadow walking toward me through the misty vapour. I felt Archie tense, but before I could ask him any questions, the shadow turned into a man.

I heard him give a huff of laughter, one that was so familiar. Tears sprang to my eyes. He stepped closer and I could smell him, sweat and cologne and Owen. He wasn't quite substantial, although more solid than he had been in the window of the clothing store.

"Emilia," he said, and his voice was full of awe and amazement, and so much love.

"Owen…"

He looked along the platform. "I missed my train…I've waited for so long for another, but…I didn't think one is coming…"

"It's because Archie took your body." My throat was aching with emotion but I was resolute. "Your soul can't move on. That's what McIvor told me."

Owen spoke quietly. "And now I can?" He looked uncertain. "I can leave this place?"

The train began to move slowly toward us, barely visible in the shifting steam. I felt as if it was stalking us. As if Owen was its prey. He took a step toward it.

"No!" I meant to shout but I couldn't find my breath.

"Let him go," Archie said urgently. "He wants to go, so let him. I'm the one who wants to live."

Owen looked to me, hesitating. "I died, Emilia. I can't come back from that. I want to come with you, but I died."

"Archie came back!"

"And look how that worked out?" he said gently. He reached out, as if he wasn't quite sure of himself, and touched my cheek. His fingertips felt like a breath of cool air against my skin.

"Owen, please…"

But Archie wasn't going to stand in silence and listen to us. "You're going to jail for kidnapping, and sooner or later the *Courier* is going to find the holes in the story I gave them about your 'return'. You'll be disgraced, no one will employ you. What sort of life can you give to Emilia then?"

I looked at Archie in shock. He had agreed to willing trade places with Owen, but I saw then that Owen had to be willing too. Archie was trying to change his mind.

I spoke urgently. "McIvor cheated. He made certain you died, and then he used your body for Archie. If he hadn't done that then you would have moved on from this place. Instead you are stuck here, where you shouldn't be."

He thought a moment. "Are there rules to this madness then?"

"Yes, yes, there are. And McIvor broke them. Come with me. Please, Owen."

The doubt in his eyes wavered.

"McIvor took me instead," Archie said angrily, "because you were dilly dallying, just as you are now! Worrying about Emilia instead of yourself. When he made you the offer to bring you back you said 'No' but I was right there, and I said 'Yes'."

Owen's eyes were on my face, and I could see the doubt and worry fighting with the longing to do as I said.

"Come with me," I said again. "Come home, Owen."

He opened his mouth to answer, before his eyes slid past me and widened. His breath hitched and

Archie swore. They were both staring behind me, and when I turned I saw the train was right there.

The door to the carriages swung open and a conductor stepped out. Tall and thin, his face bone white, he looked from Owen to Archie and back again. My heart was beating too hard, too fast, as if my body knew this wasn't a real person, a real conductor. My mind had reconstructed him into something familiar, to spare me, but the ancient part of my brain knew he was something else altogether.

"Ticket, sirs," the conductor said.

He considered Archie with his dark gaze, then reached out and pulled a ticket from his upper breast pocket. "There it is. Come along now."

Archie was wild eyed. With a cry, he snatched the ticket back and tore it into pieces, but before he was done the conductor reached into his pocket and pull out another. Archie didn't seem to know what to do. He went to turn, probably to run, but the conductor took hold of his arm and Archie stilled.

"Now sir, don't be like that. You need to get aboard. The train is waiting."

Archie shook his head, tugging at the conductor's grip, but it was evidently too strong for him to break. "No! I won't!"

In an instant, smoke swirled about him, thickening. It was as if it caught him up in its coils and held him fast. Archie screamed, fighting, but the smoke lifted him and deposited him through the door and into the train. The sound of his voice faded, as Owen and I stood frozen with horror.

The conductor looked at Owen. "We've met before, haven't we? Do you have your ticket yet, sir?"

Owen reached down into his breast pocket and I held my breath. He glanced at me and then at the conductor. "I can't find it. I… I don't have it."

The conductor nodded slowly. "Never mind, sir. I'm sure you'll be able to catch a later train." He turned away, and climbed back inside. Slowly the engine began to move away, the carriages drawn with it. Briefly, through one of the windows, we saw Archie. He was pounding soundlessly on the glass, his mouth opening and shutting. He looked terrified because he knew there was no escape for him, not this time. And perhaps he was well aware that, wherever he was going, there would be a reckoning for his misdeeds.

The sound of the departing train faded into silence, and we were alone on the ruined platform. Owen and me.

TWENTY-FOUR

I REPEATED ALOUD MCIVOR'S earlier instructions to me.

During your journey you must not turn back to look at Owen. Not even once. Not even a glance. If you do, then all your efforts will be wasted and he will be flung back into the realm of lost souls

"Orpheus and Eurydice? Are you sure?" Owen sounded sceptical.

"I won't look," I promised, my voice determined, but shaky.

"I'll be right behind you." He sounded grim. He took my hand in his, holding it for a moment, and although it was cold I felt the warmth of him. That was when he noticed the scar on my wrist. His eyes widened. "Emilia?"

"I know. I had to. It was the only way. I'm tethered to McIvor and that bond is how we will get out of here."

"Did...did Robinson have one too?"

"Yes. It means McIvor owned him, body and soul."

"I don't have one," Owen said thoughtfully, "because I refused his offer."

"You refused him?" I tried not to think that

Owen had a chance to come home and he'd said no. "Is that what Archie meant? When you were both on the platform and McIvor appeared?"

"Yes. He would have owned me, Emilia, and through me, he would have owned you. I knew I couldn't let him. He is a bad man. Evil. So I said no, and then the chap beside me jumped up and said he would agree instead. It was Archie Robinson."

"He took advantage of the offer to you. And McIvor agreed."

"Yes."

So it hadn't been a mistake after all, unlike Colonel Peters or the others Anna had hinted at. McIvor had targeted Owen on purpose, made him the offer of life, and it was Owen's refusal that brought Archie back in his stead.

"What will we do when we get away from here?" My voice was shakier than ever. "About McIvor?"

He must have understood how precarious my position was. Even if we made it back to the surface safely, McIvor would still own me. "One thing at a time," he said quietly. "Off we go. That's it. Slowly, carefully, we'll get there. And Emilia?"

"Yes?" I whispered, my back turned to him.

"I love you."

The tears that had stung my eyes were now warm on my cheeks. I didn't know if they were real or a manifestation of the joy and anxiety I now felt. Whatever they were, I brushed them away as best I could, and began to walk back the way Archie and I had come.

Archie… where was he now? I let the stray thought go. He was gone and Owen was here, behind me, and it was imperative we reach the surface.

I had been so full of my own thoughts I had not noticed the narrow silver cord now attached to the scar on my wrist. It looped away into the darkness, showing me the direction I must travel. This was my tether, the connection between my soul and my body, still seated with Anna in the room in London. And I understood now that this was how McIvor controlled those souls he chose to bring back. He had only to cut the tether and their souls would return here, and the very threat of that would keep them obedient. Was that how he would attempt to control me? All the same, I was very grateful for the guiding thread of light.

We had left No Man's Land behind and were inside a tunnel. It sloped up in total darkness, apart from my tether. I couldn't even see the entrance to the surface and I dared not turn to look for the lights of the station. I placed each foot carefully, not wanting to fall.

Anna had told me that I had to make this journey back on my own, without help from her or McIvor. The tethering would help me, guide me, but it was up to me to get Owen's soul safely home.

Now the tunnel had opened out into a large cave. Wide enough that the edges were indistinct. Shadowy. I could see shapes though, twisting and moving through the shadows. I hoped, whatever the creatures were, they would not approach us. I had no magic tricks or spells to keep us safe from them. The air hummed with their presence, and then they began to wail. Horrible, heart-breaking sounds, that sent chills down my spine.

"They sound distraught," Owen said from behind me. "But I don't think they mean *us* any harm."

I hoped he was right. The sounds were truly awful, and sad too. Were these lost souls, unable to find their way out of this place? Were they like Owen, trapped in limbo with no escape? I shuddered at the thought.

"I still don't like them," I said. "We need to get through this cave."

I had hardly spoken when a whisper came out of the nothingness. "*Emilia.*"

I stopped. Warm breath brushed against my cheek and I shivered, flinching away.

"What is it?" Owen spoke from behind me. "Emilia, what's wrong?"

"There's someone else with us."

"Who? Is it McIvor?"

"I don't know."

The wailing around us stopped and there was a sinister chuckle. I took a step forward, and then another, determined to ignore whoever it was. I almost preferred it to be McIvor, at least I understood his brand of malevolence.

The whisper came again. "How can you be sure that's Owen behind you?"

"What do you mean?" I answered despite myself.

"It could be someone else. It could be Archie."

A spike of anxiety halted me again. Could that be true? Would I find, when we got to the surface, that it was Archie who had been following me and Owen was still abandoned?

"You'll know if you look at him," came that whisper in my ear. "*Look* at him."

Whoever the whisper belonged to was feeding my temptation, urging me to take one little look… And if I did…

"Owen is still down there. You've left him behind."

"No," I said.

"How can you be sure? Just one little peep."

I almost turned. I think I would have turned.

Owen's voice stopped me. "I can't hear what he's saying, but I can guess. You are thinking I am someone else. Tell me, Emilia, is the Remington still tucked away at your father's? You know, you really should be using it. Does the 'g' key still stick?"

Relief overwhelmed me. I gasped out a laugh. It was him, it had to be.

We started off again and finally the cave came to an end, and to my relief we seemed to have left the whisperer behind.

But before long the tunnel opened out again, into another cave. This one was full of sound and ghostly images. The silver cord from my wrist twisted between the figures, so that we had to walk among them. Far closer than I would have liked. However I soon realised that the ghosts couldn't see us. They were lost in conversation with themselves or somebody I couldn't see.

Some of them seemed to have been injured—I could see the bandages and even open wounds. At one point the figures were massed so thickly I had to push through them. It was like walking through water. But they still seemed oblivious. Lost in their own worlds.

"I think they are alive, at least their bodies are, but their souls are here," Owen said from behind me. "Hospital patients, perhaps? People in comas who are not dead, but neither are they alive."

It seemed as good an explanation as any.

Once again I was glad to escape the strange crowd, and once again we found ourselves in yet another cave.

Figures drifted, some floating, others walking. Their eyes were open but most of them did not seem to see us. One or two stared, and occasionally one of them would disappear with a pop, like a soap bubble bursting and leaving nothing behind. As if they had awoken.

I guessed this was the realm of dreams that McIvor had told me about. The final stop before we were back in the land of the living.

My relief was short lived because the whisperer had returned.

"You are bringing Archie back into the world. Perhaps you prefer him, Emilia."

I did not respond, I kept walking, praying that Owen was still behind me.

"Maybe you like a man who is a little rough? Owen is such a gentleman, isn't he? Not like Archie."

I felt my cheeks burn with shame and bit back

the protests on my lips. Behind me there was silence. I slowed my steps and stopped, desperate to turn, to see Owen's face, to tell him it wasn't true.

"Emilia, you need to keep walking," he said quietly.

"If it was a choice between Owen and Archie, there would never be a question as to who I would choose," I said aloud. "Are you listening whoever you are?"

There was a vile chuckle. I was sure it was McIvor. "Then you have chosen the wrong man," he said. "Look!"

Before my eyes a figure began to materialise. A tall man in uniform with dark hair, grey eyes and crooked smile. *Owen!* He reached out to me, as if to beg me to save him.

Shocked, confused, I asked myself how Owen could be there, when he was behind me? Was it true? Had Archie somehow re-entered Owen's body? Had he tricked me once again?

I almost turned. I was so close to turning.

"Emilia, stop!" Owen's urgent voice pierced through my terror. "Whatever is happening, stop and think. I am here, right here. McIvor is trying to trick you. Ignore him. Take me home, my love. Take me back to Belsham and your father, and let me live again."

My fear drained away. The vision in front of me wavered and began to dissolve. And then McIvor's face was pressed to mine. Dark eyes swallowing me up, the stench of fire stinging my nostrils.

"No!" I screamed.

"Leave her alone!" Owen shouted.

And then something very strange began to happen. Voices rose up behind us, and there was a stirring in the air, as if a mass of beings had entered the dream realm.

"McIvor? Is McIvor here?" they wailed. The refrain was taken up and repeated over and over again, growing ever louder.

I wanted to turn but knew I didn't dare. But Owen could.

"The lost souls from the first cave are here," he said. "They followed us. Followed *you*. They know I am one of them and I think they hoped you could save them too."

McIvor's eyes widened. He had heard them too, and now he saw them. "No," he said, as if it was an order. "You shouldn't be here. This isn't your place. Get back! Do as I tell you."

Could some of these souls be from McIvor's experiments? Lost, and unable to escape to either life or death? His botched efforts?

Whatever or whoever they were, they didn't obey him. The wails grew louder, and now they were angry. There was a rush of sound, like a great wind blowing through the cave, and I heard McIvor scream.

Briefly I saw his face change. He looked surprised. Then the wind stilled, and everything fell quiet, and he and the souls were gone.

My legs wobbled and I thought I was going to fall to the ground, but I couldn't do that. I still had to complete my task. So I set my gaze in front of me and started walking again. We were in another tunnel, rising slowly upward.

"Come on," I said, ignoring Owen's worried questions. "Hurry."

Whatever had happened to McIvor may only have been temporary and I couldn't risk waiting to see. I quickened my steps and just when I thought the tunnel would go on forever, I stepped out into the misty silence of No Man's Land. And saw that the sun was rising. It was like a promise of better times to come.

I broke then. I broke into a thousand pieces.

But Owen was there to hold me.

TWENTY-FIVE

ANNA WAS WAITING for us in No Man's Land. She looked even paler than before, but resolute. She took our hands, and it was only then that I noticed the scar was gone from my wrist. Like a malignant stain, the link to McIvor was gone.

Did that mean we were free of him? I tried to ask, but we were already spiralling into darkness.

Next time I woke, we were in the room above the bookshop in Tottenham Court Road. Anna was still holding my hands, but as my eyes opened she released them. The first thing I did was look across to where Archie had been sitting wearing Owen's skin, under Florence's watchful gaze. He was still there, slumped over, but as I stared, he straightened and his eyes flickered and opened. They focussed on his sister.

"Florence?" he said. "Is it you?"

"Owen? I…" Instead of throwing herself into his arms she held herself back. Her voice trembled. "What was the name of your dog? The one given to you when you were five?"

He smiled. "You mean Napoleon? Small and bossy. I still miss him."

Florence gasped and now she did throw herself into his arms.

Later, when things had calmed down, Florence took me aside.

"When you were…gone," she said, "McIvor went into a trance too. Anna said he was trying to stop you from bringing Owen back. That he was more interested in placing your soul in another body and observing what would happen."

Seeing my shocked face, Florence hurried on. "Anna was distraught. And then suddenly McIvor just fell down. He was just…dead."

I knew why that was. The lost souls from his experiments had taken their revenge upon him.

I had no pity for McIvor.

"He was an evil man."

Anna was standing behind us. She had followed and overheard Florence. She looked ten years older than when we had started this.

With the doctor gone, there were still many questions we could not answer, and perhaps we never would. We walked through the rooms, seeking clues. I went back to the room with the jars and their horrid contents, and in a smaller room next door we found a surgery. A dissection table and sharp instruments, and more of the damnable jars. A cabinet held what might have been souvenirs. They were rather like the ones in Archie's box. Cigarette cases and rings, a pipe and various photographs of men and women.

I didn't know any of them but Anna did. Her mouth tightened and she turned away.

On the wall were framed certificates. They

covered over a hundred years, each one from a medical school or hospital with the name 'McIvor' on it. The earliest was from the Anatomy section of a Medical School in Edinburgh and was dated 1828. It had been presented to a Dr McIvor for his work in dissection of the human body.

Had the doctor lived so long? I wondered. Or was he one in a long line of medical men? Or had his soul left when his body grew too old and found another, younger host. I didn't give my thoughts voice, but I knew Owen was thinking the same thing when we exchanged glances.

Whatever the truth it was over.

Owen squeezed my hand and suddenly I just wanted to get away from this awful place, to try to forget.

I turned to Anna. "You saved us. And you helped bring Owen home. I can never thank you enough."

For a moment her face clouded with grief, but she forced back the tears. "The man you know as McIvor wanted me to believe he saved me from a life of mediocrity. That may well have been so, but he learned from me, too. He was an eager pupil. I was afraid of him, and yet now I can't imagine my life without him."

McIvor still owned Anna, even without the scar about her wrist. I hoped that with him gone, she would break free of his evil influence.

Florence put her arm about me. "Is he gone for good?" she asked.

Anna hesitated. "Gone from this world, anyway." She smiled and the atmosphere lightened.

"Go home and live your lives. Be happy. After this you deserve it."

EPILOGUE

10 months later

FLORENCE STOOD BESIDE me, her arms wrapped tight around her waist, staring at the door to the prison. After the events of Tottenham Court Road, she had sat Eddie down and told him everything. She said she couldn't keep secrets from him. He had listened to her in silence, struggling not to argue with her. It took him many weeks, and many repeats of the story, before he began to accept. I think he realised that even if he found such matters far beyond his experience, he was willing to suspend his disbelief for Florence's sake.

Beside me, Maggie skipped about in her new shoes, humming under her breath. I had fulfilled my promise to Archie Robinson and his daughter was now part of the household at Easton Street. There had been a time when I wondered if the past might prove too difficult for her to overcome, but children are resilient. She was attending school and had made friends, and to my surprise my father seemed to have developed a soft spot for the girl. During our visits to Belsham, he set aside whatever work he was doing and smiled as she chattered away to him as if they had known each other all their lives.

Owen had served his six months for assault and was about to be released.

After he had returned to the land of the living, he was ill for a long time. Lying in the hospital and raving. I had travelled to Hades and back to save him, only to almost lose him to the last wave of the Spanish flu. Gradually he began to recover, but our relief didn't last long. He was taken away to jail to serve his sentence. Although six months seemed little enough for what Archie had done to Bertha.

I wasn't sure what sort of life we would have together. Because of Archie, Owen lost his job at the *Courier*, and he lost many of his friends. Would Owen think this new chance at life worth it if he couldn't do what he loved? I wondered if he ever regretted me bringing him back.

"Here he is," Florence said. She managed a tense smile.

Owen had come through the prison door and now he lifted his face, squinting in the light. He looked thinner, his skin paler, and his dark hair messy. After a long and deep breath, he looked around until he found us.

I saw his mouth curl up in that lopsided grin. I knew then. Even before he came to a breathless halt in front of us, I knew what he would say. It *was* worth it. And I would do it again and again just to have him back.

"Emilia," he said, his voice low, fighting tears. "Florence."

Florence stared up at him, her eyes wide. And then flung herself into his arms.

He held her tight, and a tear ran down my cheek.

He reached out an arm for me and I stepped in, pressing my face to his chest. He smelt of hard days and longer nights, and he had a long recovery ahead of him. But none of that mattered—he was alive.

Maggie was a little less enthusiastic, because she remembered the other Owen who had hurt her mother. I held tight to her hand, and knew that in time she would accept this man was one to trust and love.

I wasn't sure what life in the short term held for us. What would we do? Go back to Belsham? My father would welcome us, of course. We could rest there, recover and take stock and consider the future. The miracle was that we had a future. Together.

McIvor and Archie, even Anna, were part of a past I did not want to revisit. We had been granted the chance to start again.

And that meant everything.

MESSAGE FROM THE AUTHOR

Thank you for reading *With My Last Breath,* my gothic spooky book.

I began work on this book just before the pandemic, and what seemed like a good idea at the time wasn't so well received once we were in lock-down. However I loved the idea so much I kept writing, and I am glad I did. I still love the story and I'd be interested to know what you think.

Many thanks to those who helped me along the way, in particular Noah Chin for editing that went far and beyond, and Sandy for agreeing to read the book over Christmas 2023. Christine's enthusiasm in the early days kept me writing, as well as her thorough copy editing.

Although I have carefully researched the period the book is set in, any mistakes are entirely mine.

If you enjoyed the book you may consider leaving an honest review.

Thank you!

AUTHOR BIO

Kaye Dobbie has been writing professionally ever since she won the Big River short story contest at the age of eighteen. Her career has undergone many changes, including writing Australian historical fiction under the name Lilly Sommers, to romance written as Sara Bennett and published in the US and Australia. Her books have been nominated for a number of awards and translated into many languages. As Kaye Dobbie she is published in Australia and Germany. Kaye lives on the central Victorian goldfields, where she creates her stories despite the demands of three privileged cats. You can find her at *https://www.kayedobbie.com/*

OTHER BOOKS BY KAYE DOBBIE

The Glass House
The Bond
The Dark Dream
When Shadows Fall
Whispers from the Past
Footsteps in an Empty Room
Colours of Gold
Sweet Wattle Creek
Mackenzie Crossing
Willow Tree Bend
The Road to Ironbark
Keepers of the Lighthouse

BOOKS PREVIOUSLY WRITTEN AS DEBORAH MILES

A Passing Fancy
Sweet Mary Anne
Jealous Hearts

www.ingramcontent.com/pod-product-compliance
Lightning Source LLC
LaVergne TN
LVHW021656060526
838200LV00050B/2384